LEGO® NINJAGO

Masters of Spinjitzu

MASK OF THE SENSEI

PAPERCUT Z™

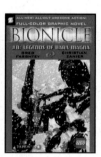

#2 MASK OF THE SENSEI

GREG FARSHTEY ★ Writer
PAULO HENRIQUE ★ Artist
LAURIE E. SMITH ★ Colorist

New York

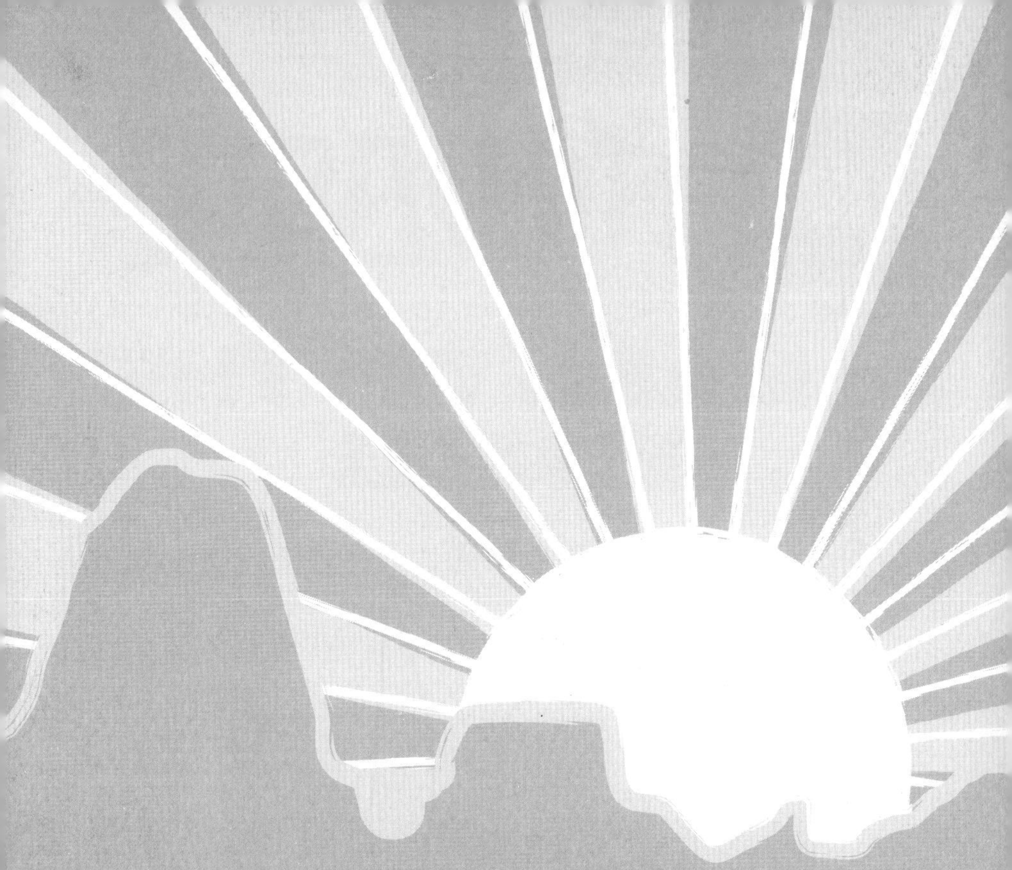

LEGO® NINJAGO Masters of Spinjitzu
#2 "Mask of the Sensei"

GREG FARSHTEY – Writer
PAULO HENRIQUE – Artist
LAURIE E. SMITH – Colorist
BRYAN SENKA – Letterer

Production by Nelson Design Group, LLC
Associate Editor – MICHAEL PETRANEK
JIM SALICRUP
Editor-in-Chief

ISBN: 978-1-59707-310-3 paperback edition
ISBN: 978-1-59707-311-0 hardcover edition

Printed in the US
March 2012 by Lifetouch Printing
5126 Forest Hills Ctt.
Loves Park, IL 61111

Distributed by Macmillan

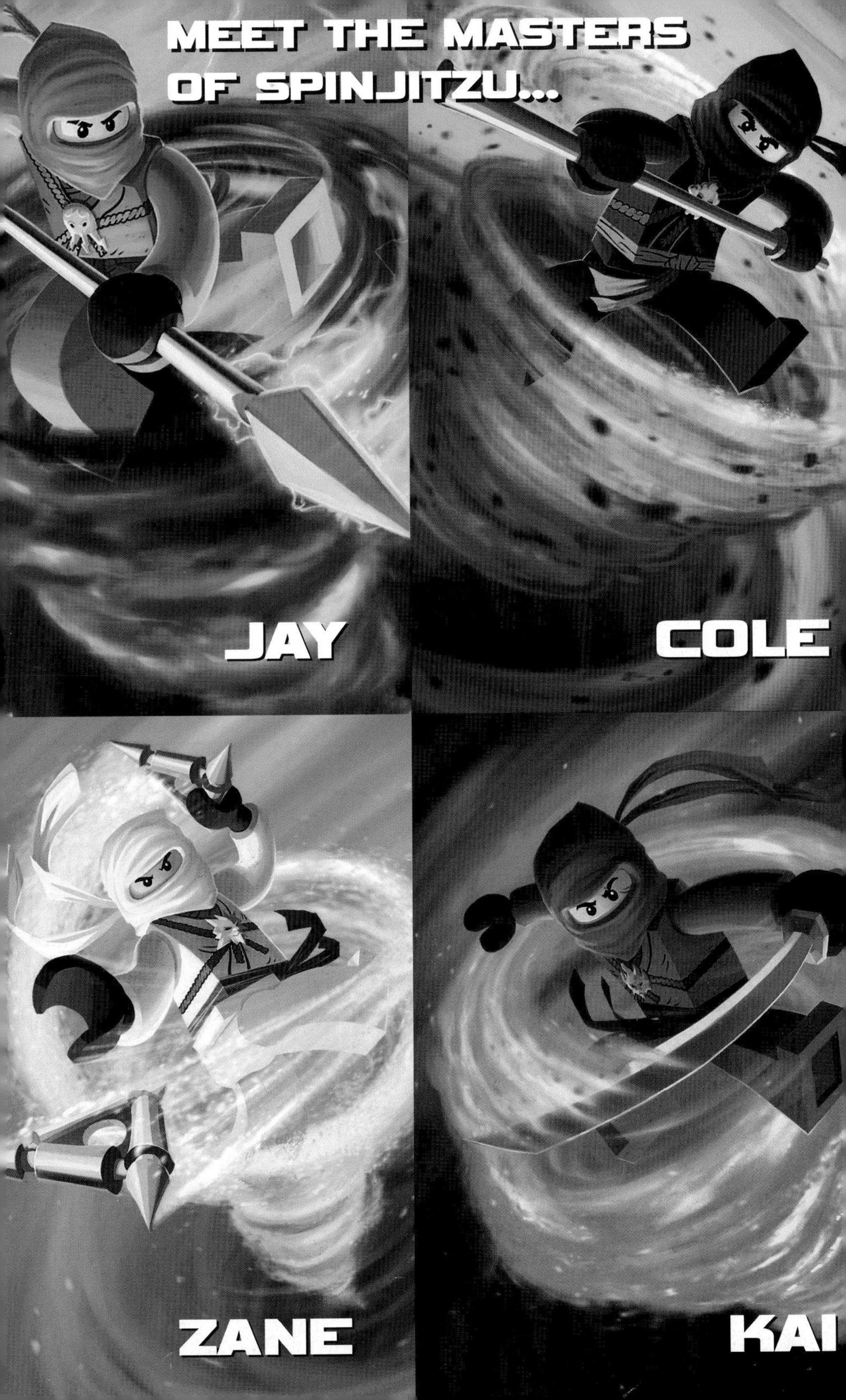
MEET THE MASTERS
OF SPINJITZU...
JAY
COLE
ZANE
KAI

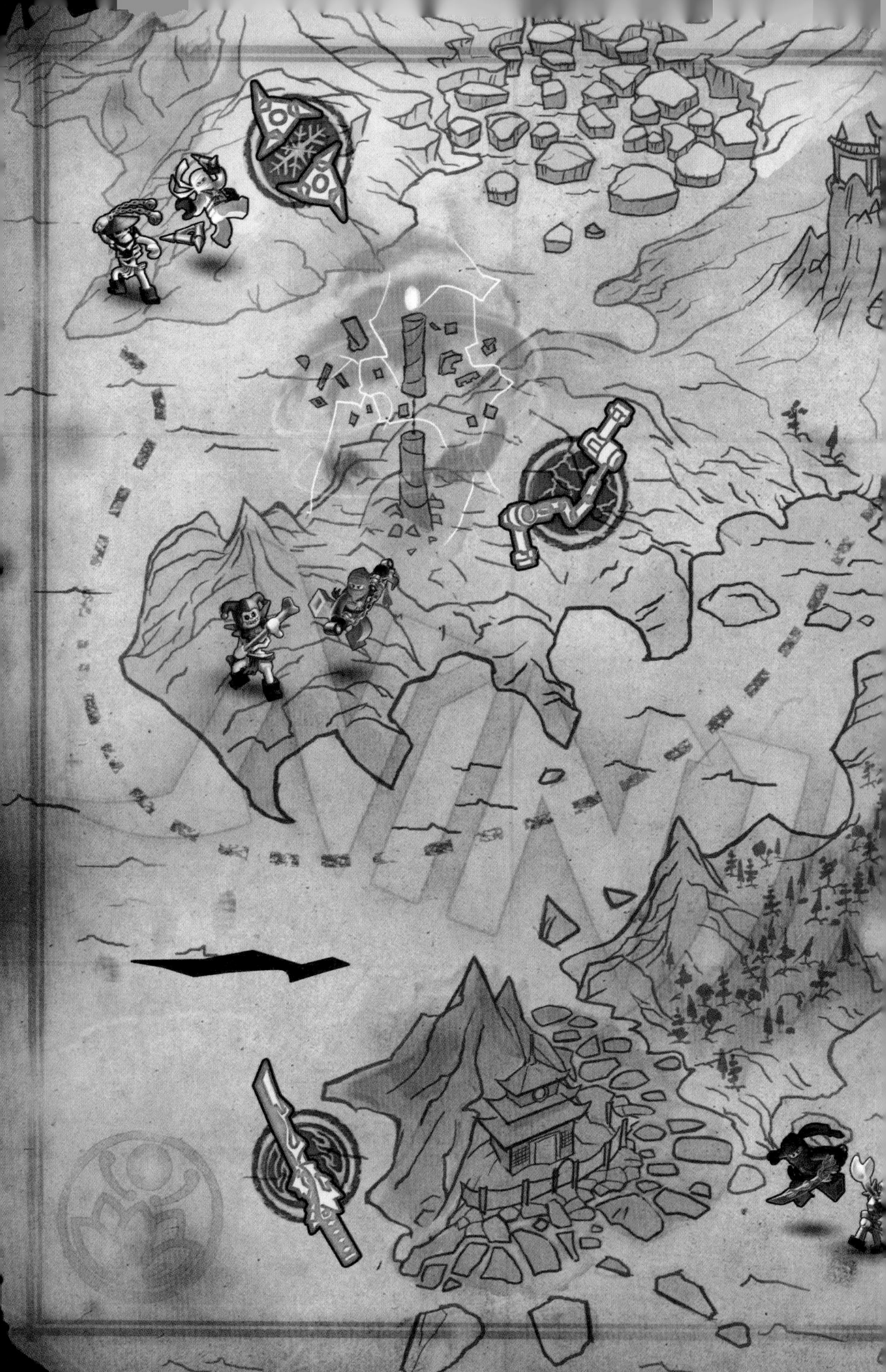

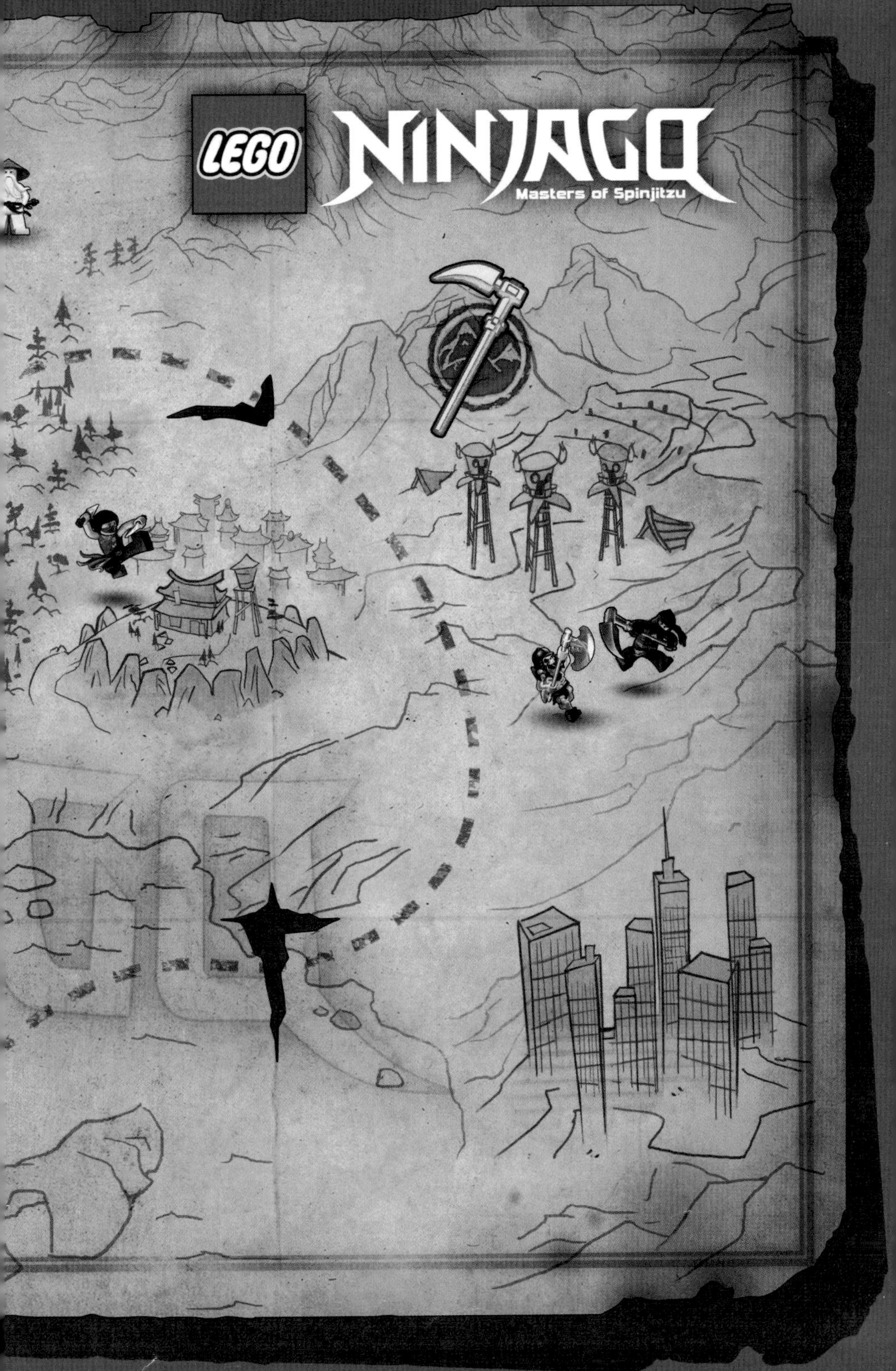
LEGO
NINJAGO
Masters of Spinjitzu

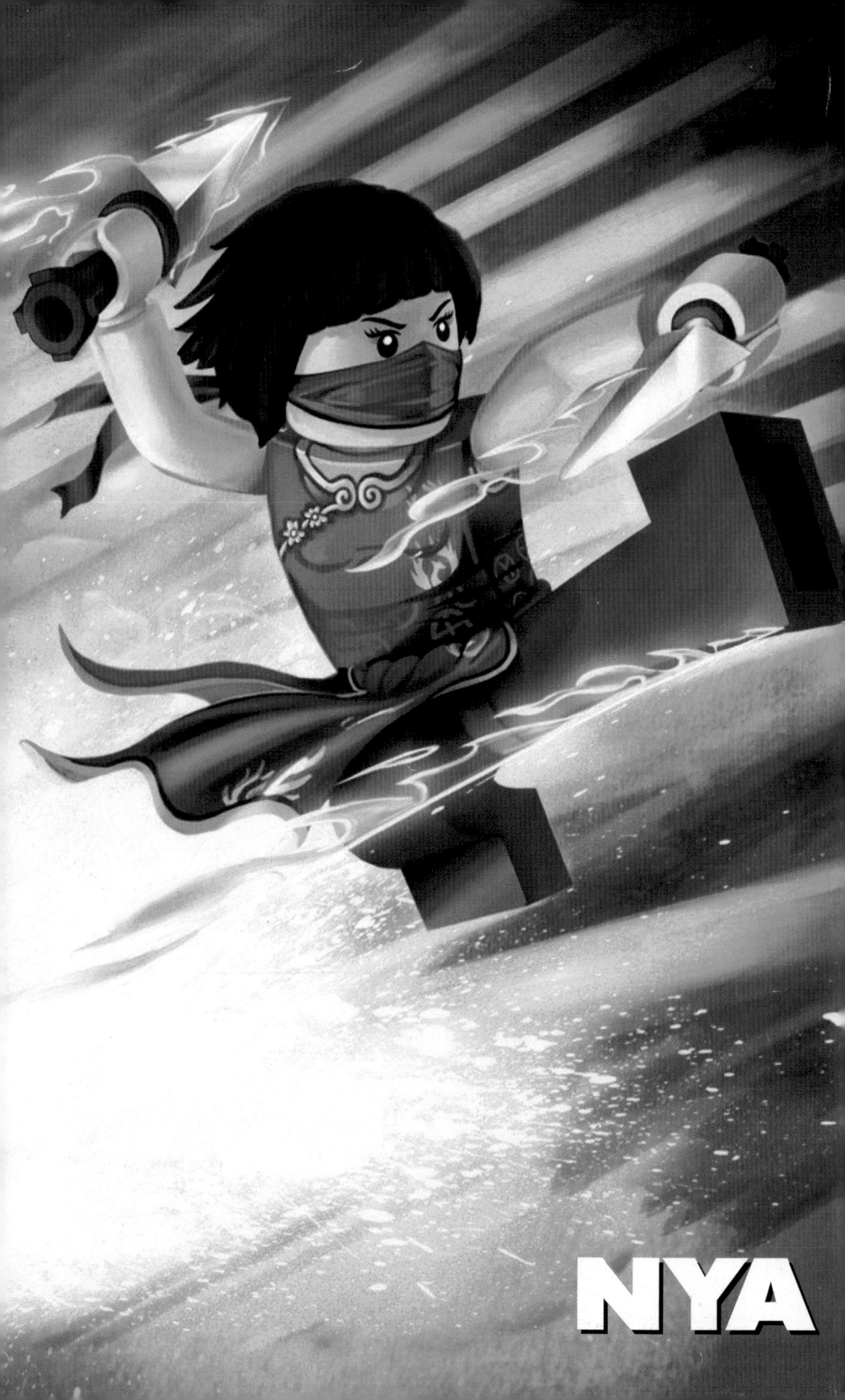
NYA

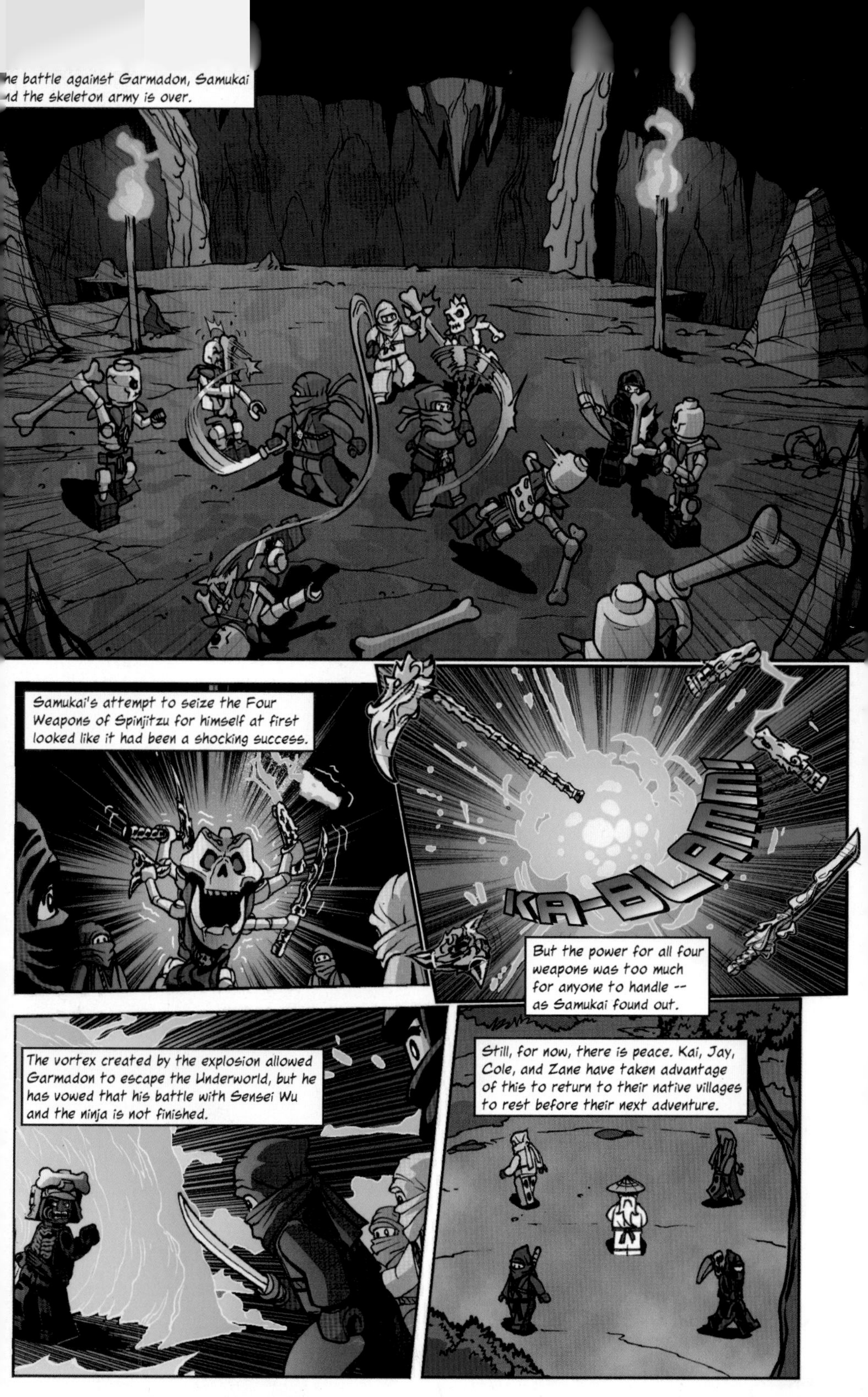
he battle against Garmadon, Samukai
nd the skeleton army is over.
Samukai's attempt to seize the Four Weapons of Spinjitzu for himself at first looked like it had been a shocking success.
KA-BLAM!
But the power for all four weapons was too much for anyone to handle -- as Samukai found out.
The vortex created by the explosion allowed Garmadon to escape the Underworld, but he has vowed that his battle with Sensei Wu and the ninja is not finished.
Still, for now, there is peace. Kai, Jay, Cole, and Zane have taken advantage of this to return to their native villages to rest before their next adventure.

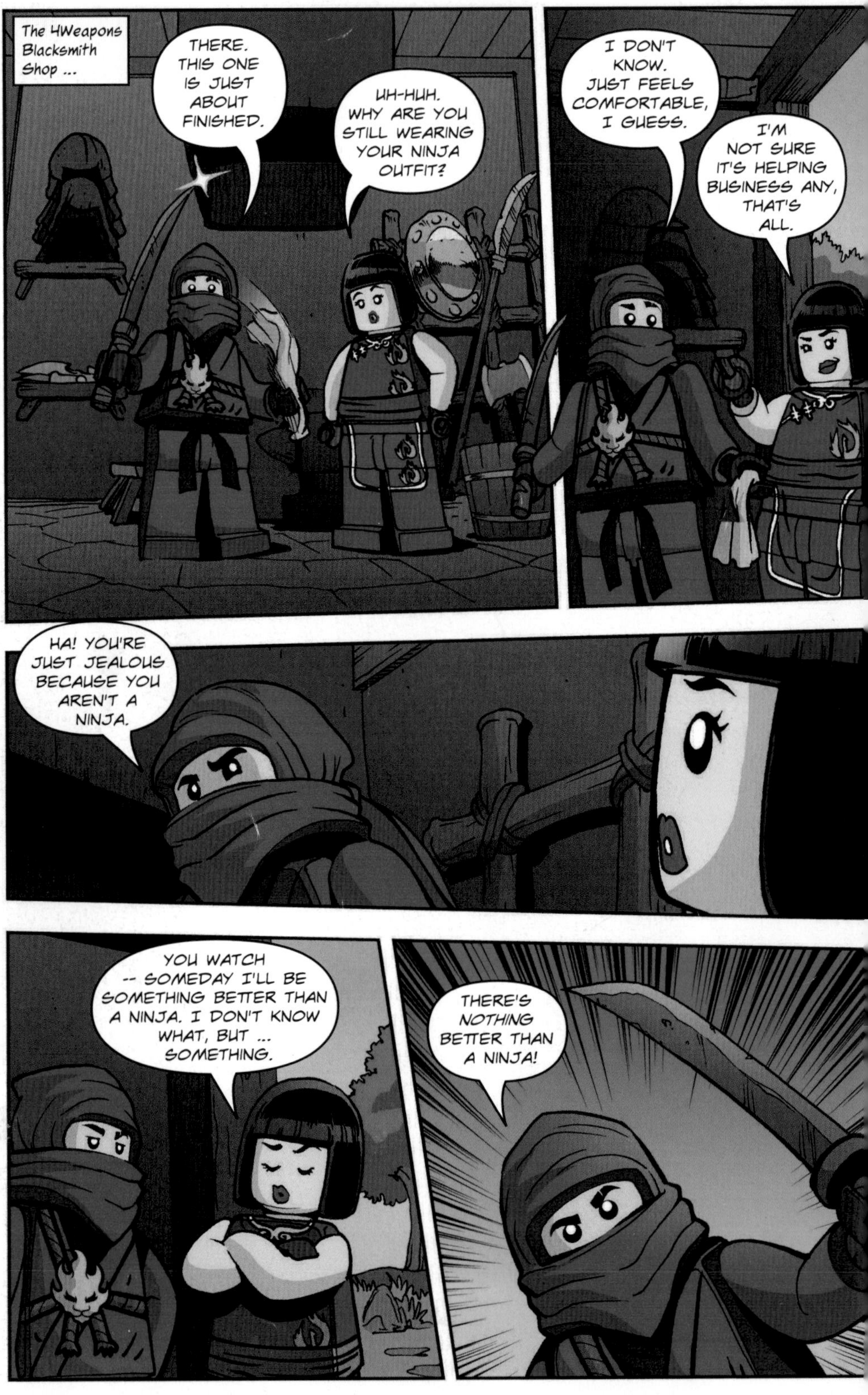
The 4Weapons Blacksmith Shop ...
THERE. THIS ONE IS JUST ABOUT FINISHED.
UH-HUH. WHY ARE YOU STILL WEARING YOUR NINJA OUTFIT?
I DON'T KNOW. JUST FEELS COMFORTABLE, I GUESS.
I'M NOT SURE IT'S HELPING BUSINESS ANY, THAT'S ALL.
HA! YOU'RE JUST JEALOUS BECAUSE YOU AREN'T A NINJA.
YOU WATCH -- SOMEDAY I'LL BE SOMETHING BETTER THAN A NINJA. I DON'T KNOW WHAT, BUT ... SOMETHING.
THERE'S *NOTHING* BETTER THAN A NINJA!

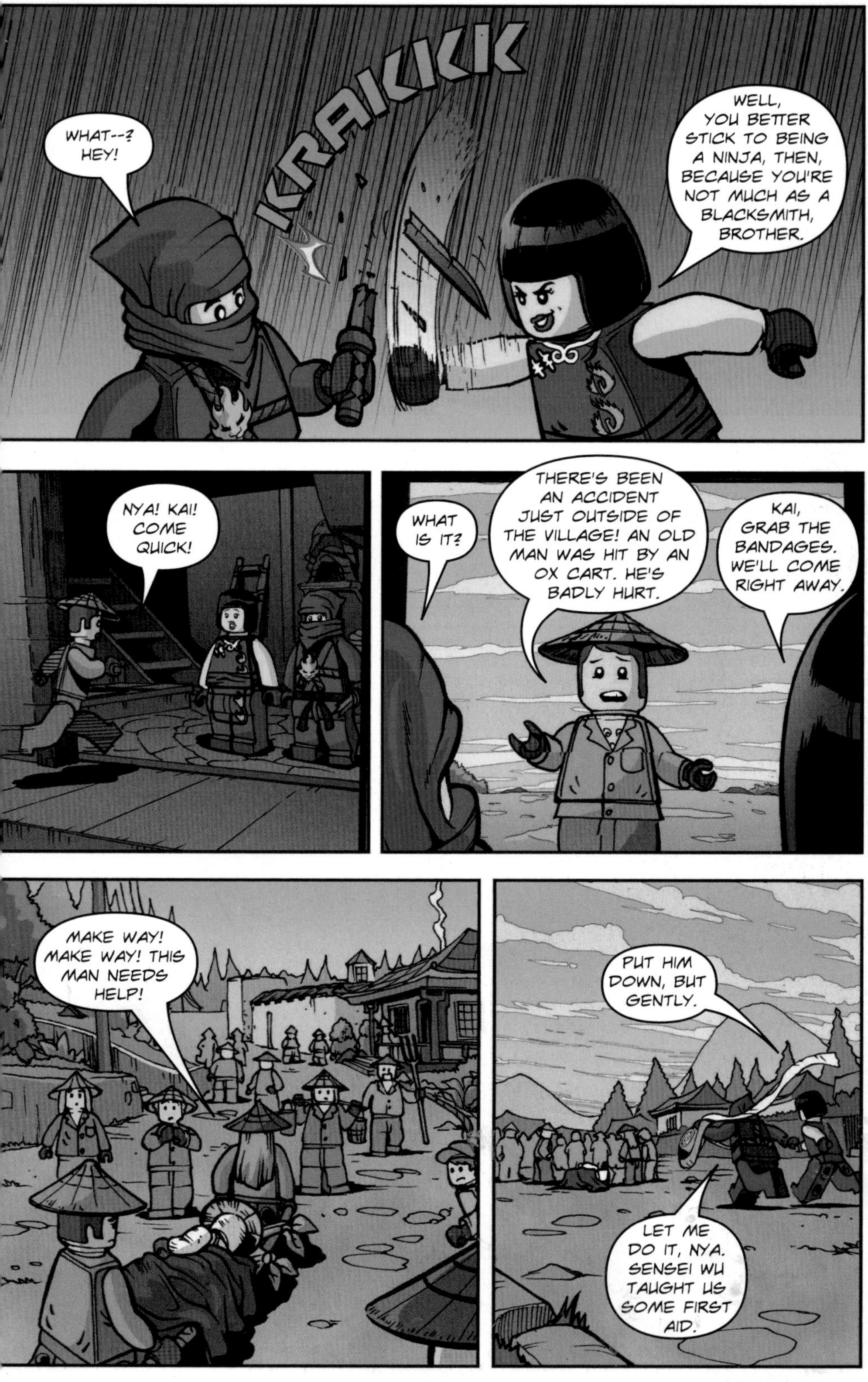
KRAKKK
WHAT--? HEY!
WELL, YOU BETTER STICK TO BEING A NINJA, THEN, BECAUSE YOU'RE NOT MUCH AS A BLACKSMITH, BROTHER.
NYA! KAI! COME QUICK!
WHAT IS IT?
THERE'S BEEN AN ACCIDENT JUST OUTSIDE OF THE VILLAGE! AN OLD MAN WAS HIT BY AN OX CART. HE'S BADLY HURT.
KAI, GRAB THE BANDAGES. WE'LL COME RIGHT AWAY.
MAKE WAY! MAKE WAY! THIS MAN NEEDS HELP!
PUT HIM DOWN, BUT GENTLY.
LET ME DO IT, NYA. SENSEI WU TAUGHT US SOME FIRST AID.

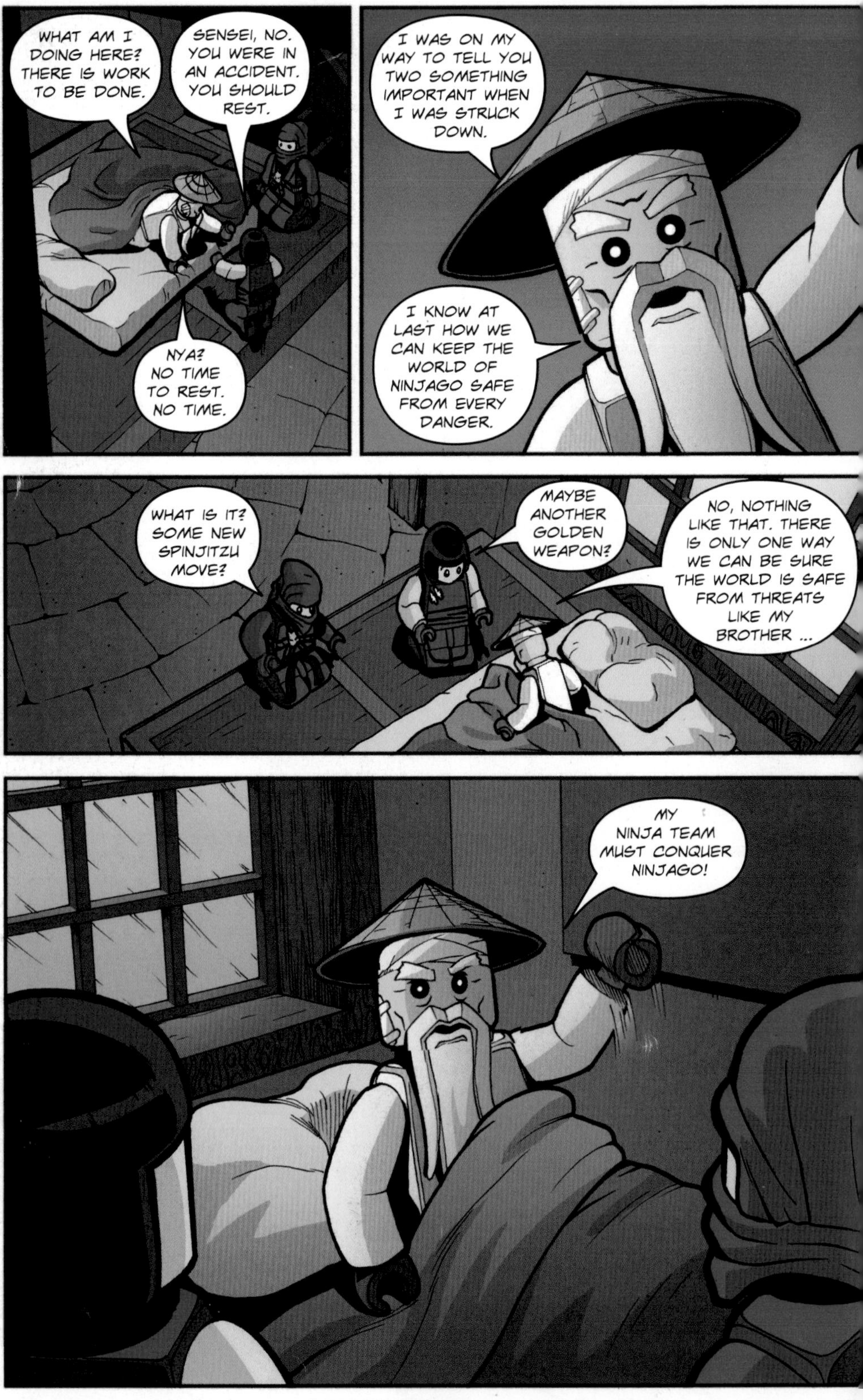
WHAT AM I DOING HERE? THERE IS WORK TO BE DONE.
SENSEI, NO. YOU WERE IN AN ACCIDENT. YOU SHOULD REST.
NYA? NO TIME TO REST. NO TIME.
I WAS ON MY WAY TO TELL YOU TWO SOMETHING IMPORTANT WHEN I WAS STRUCK DOWN.
I KNOW AT LAST HOW WE CAN KEEP THE WORLD OF NINJAGO SAFE FROM EVERY DANGER.
WHAT IS IT? SOME NEW SPINJITZU MOVE?
MAYBE ANOTHER GOLDEN WEAPON?
NO, NOTHING LIKE THAT. THERE IS ONLY ONE WAY WE CAN BE SURE THE WORLD IS SAFE FROM THREATS LIKE MY BROTHER ...
MY NINJA TEAM MUST CONQUER NINJAGO!

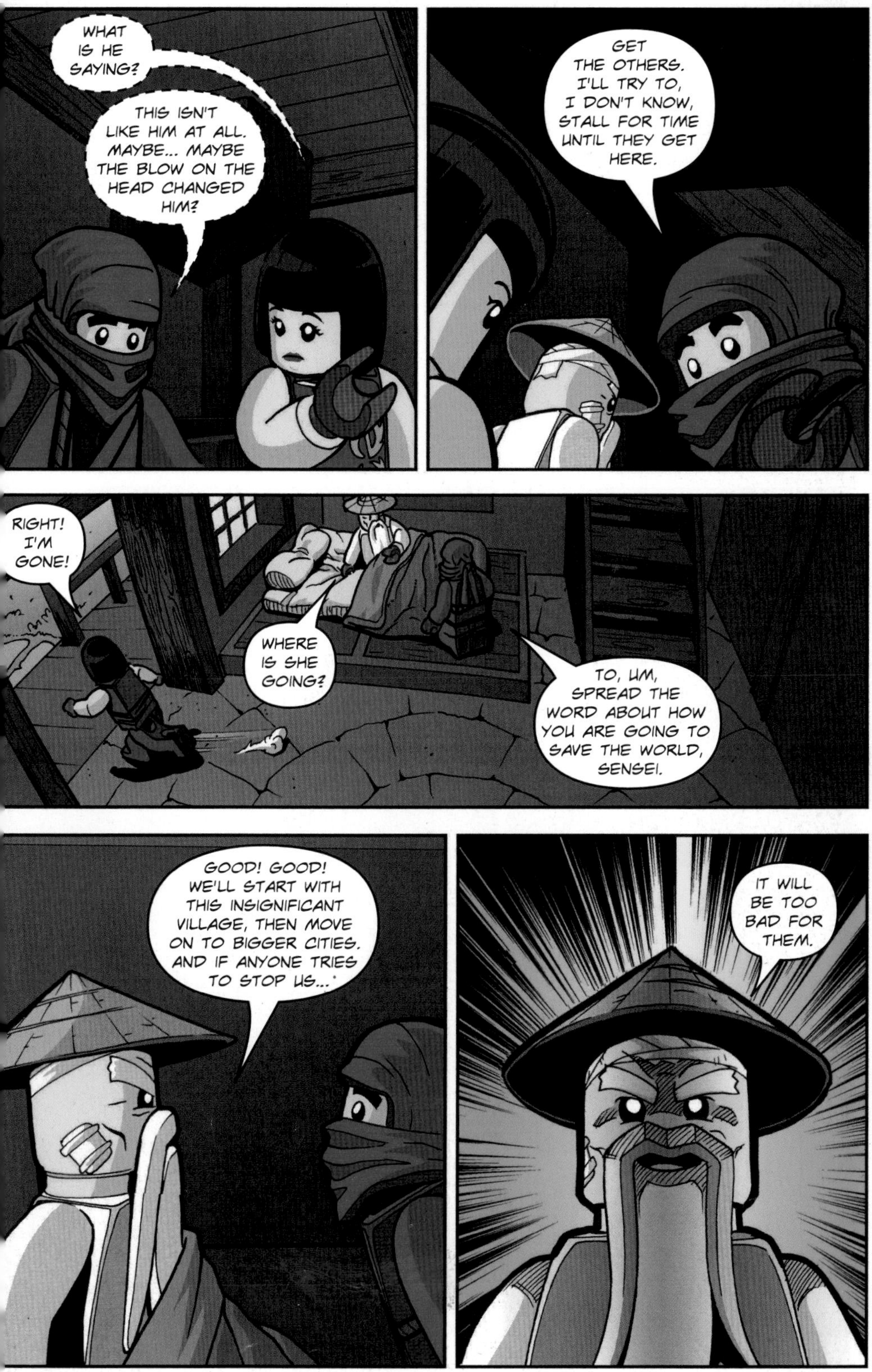
WHAT IS HE SAYING?
THIS ISN'T LIKE HIM AT ALL. MAYBE... MAYBE THE BLOW ON THE HEAD CHANGED HIM?
GET THE OTHERS. I'LL TRY TO, I DON'T KNOW, STALL FOR TIME UNTIL THEY GET HERE.
RIGHT! I'M GONE!
WHERE IS SHE GOING?
TO, UM, SPREAD THE WORD ABOUT HOW YOU ARE GOING TO SAVE THE WORLD, SENSEI.
GOOD! GOOD! WE'LL START WITH THIS INSIGNIFICANT VILLAGE, THEN MOVE ON TO BIGGER CITIES. AND IF ANYONE TRIES TO STOP US...
IT WILL BE TOO BAD FOR THEM.

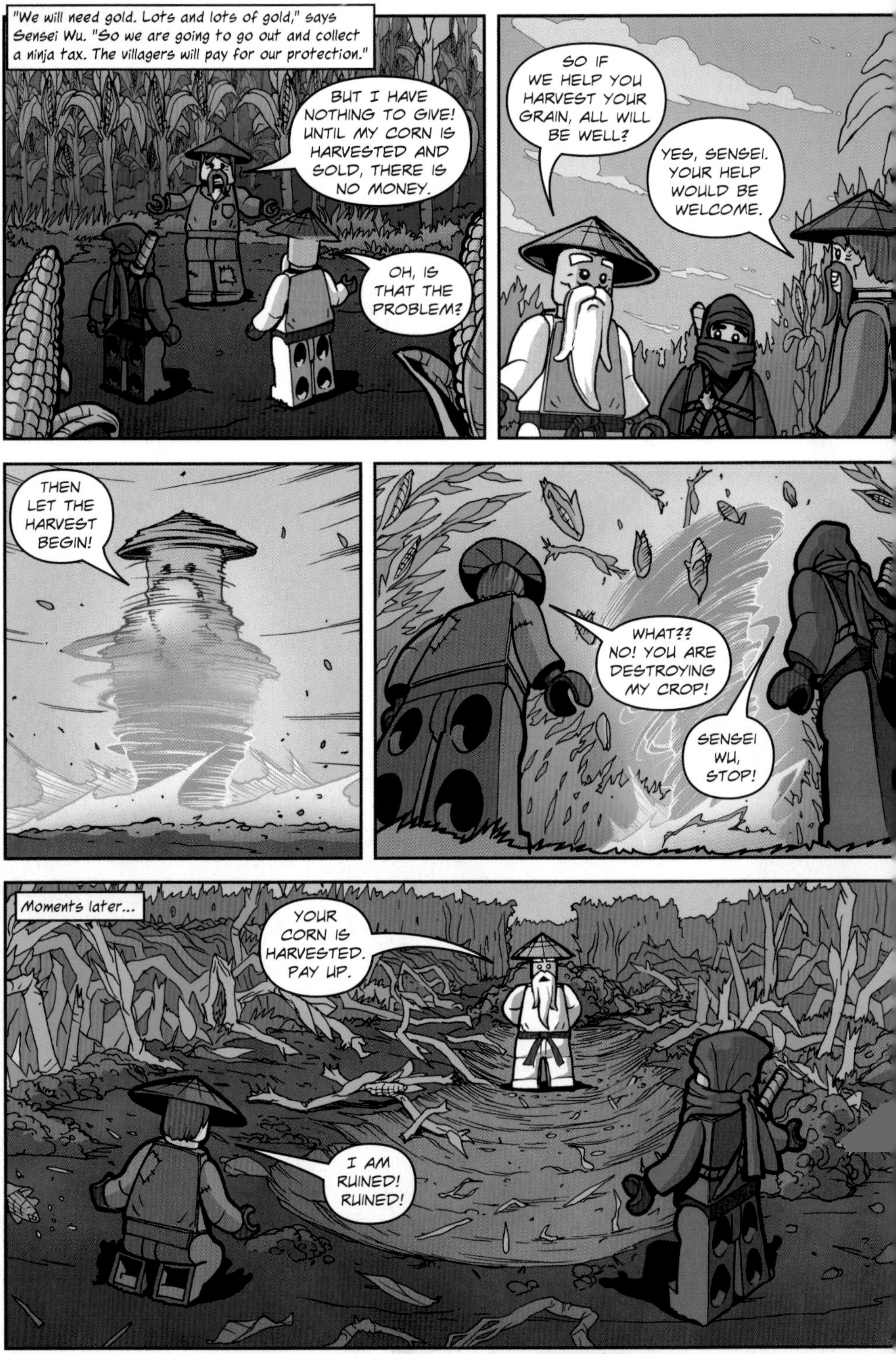
"We will need gold. Lots and lots of gold," says Sensei Wu. "So we are going to go out and collect a ninja tax. The villagers will pay for our protection."
BUT I HAVE NOTHING TO GIVE! UNTIL MY CORN IS HARVESTED AND SOLD, THERE IS NO MONEY.
OH, IS THAT THE PROBLEM?
SO IF WE HELP YOU HARVEST YOUR GRAIN, ALL WILL BE WELL?
YES, SENSEI. YOUR HELP WOULD BE WELCOME.
THEN LET THE HARVEST BEGIN!
WHAT?? NO! YOU ARE DESTROYING MY CROP!
SENSEI WU, STOP!
Moments later...
YOUR CORN IS HARVESTED. PAY UP.
I AM RUINED! RUINED!

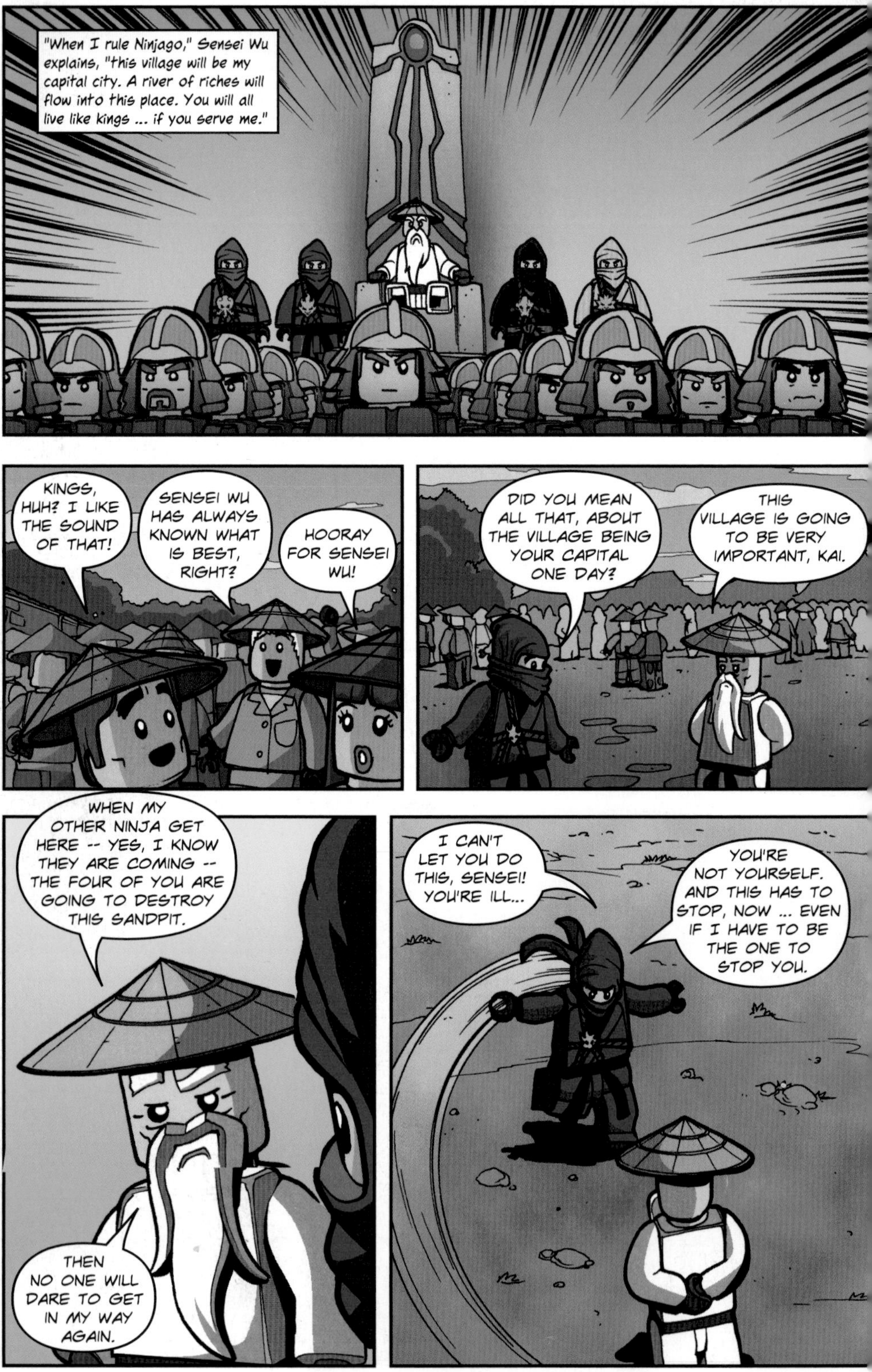
"When I rule Ninjago," Sensei Wu explains, "this village will be my capital city. A river of riches will flow into this place. You will all live like kings ... if you serve me."
KINGS, HUH? I LIKE THE SOUND OF THAT!
SENSEI WU HAS ALWAYS KNOWN WHAT IS BEST, RIGHT?
HOORAY FOR SENSEI WU!
DID YOU MEAN ALL THAT, ABOUT THE VILLAGE BEING YOUR CAPITAL ONE DAY?
THIS VILLAGE IS GOING TO BE VERY IMPORTANT, KAI.
WHEN MY OTHER NINJA GET HERE -- YES, I KNOW THEY ARE COMING -- THE FOUR OF YOU ARE GOING TO DESTROY THIS SANDPIT.
THEN NO ONE WILL DARE TO GET IN MY WAY AGAIN.
I CAN'T LET YOU DO THIS, SENSEI! YOU'RE ILL...
YOU'RE NOT YOURSELF. AND THIS HAS TO STOP, NOW ... EVEN IF I HAVE TO BE THE ONE TO STOP YOU.

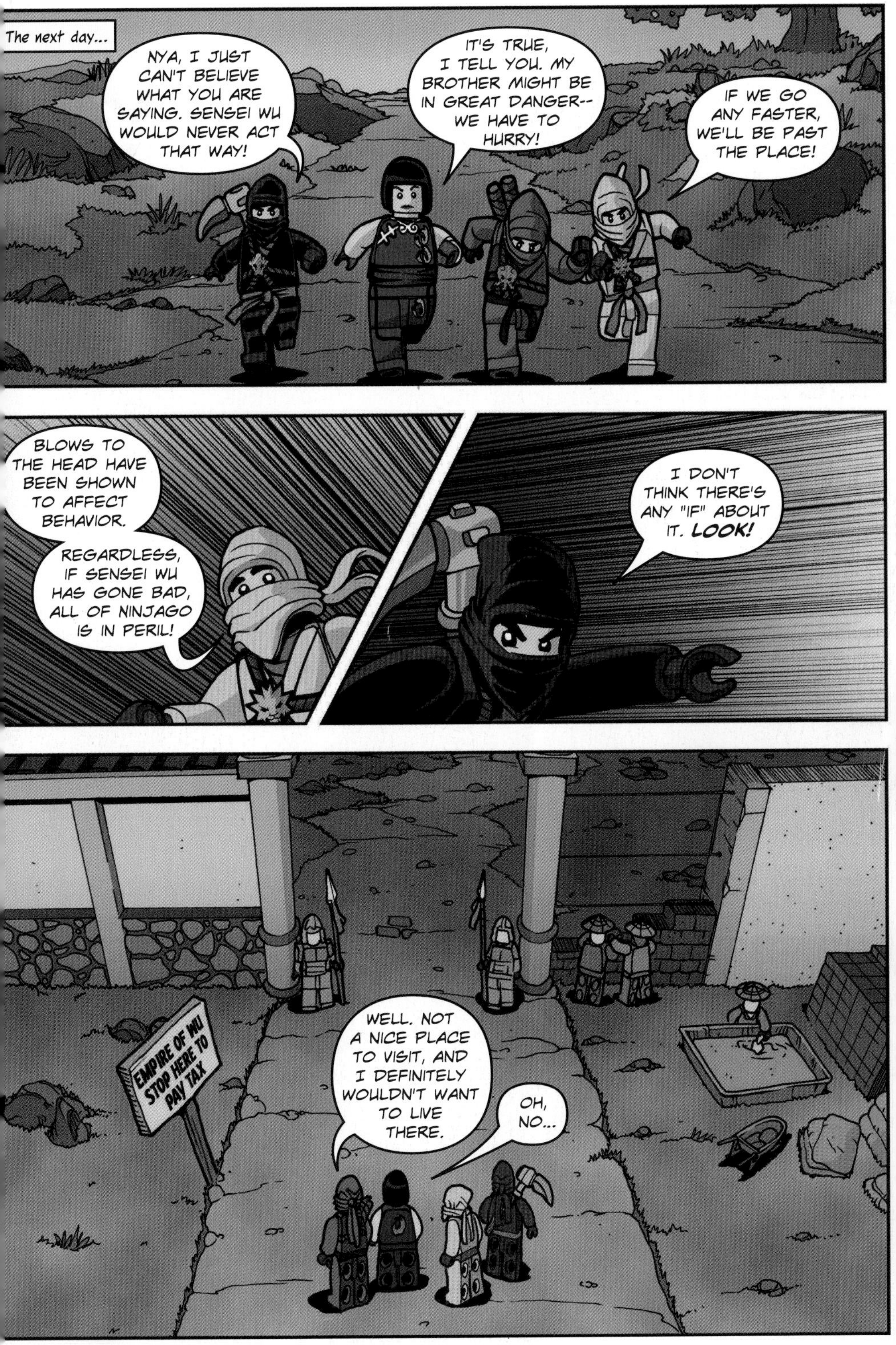
The next day...
NYA, I JUST CAN'T BELIEVE WHAT YOU ARE SAYING. SENSEI WU WOULD NEVER ACT THAT WAY!
IT'S TRUE, I TELL YOU. MY BROTHER MIGHT BE IN GREAT DANGER-- WE HAVE TO HURRY!
IF WE GO ANY FASTER, WE'LL BE PAST THE PLACE!
BLOWS TO THE HEAD HAVE BEEN SHOWN TO AFFECT BEHAVIOR.
REGARDLESS, IF SENSEI WU HAS GONE BAD, ALL OF NINJAGO IS IN PERIL!
I DON'T THINK THERE'S ANY "IF" ABOUT IT. LOOK!
EMPIRE OF WU STOP HERE TO PAY TAX
WELL. NOT A NICE PLACE TO VISIT, AND I DEFINITELY WOULDN'T WANT TO LIVE THERE.
OH, NO...

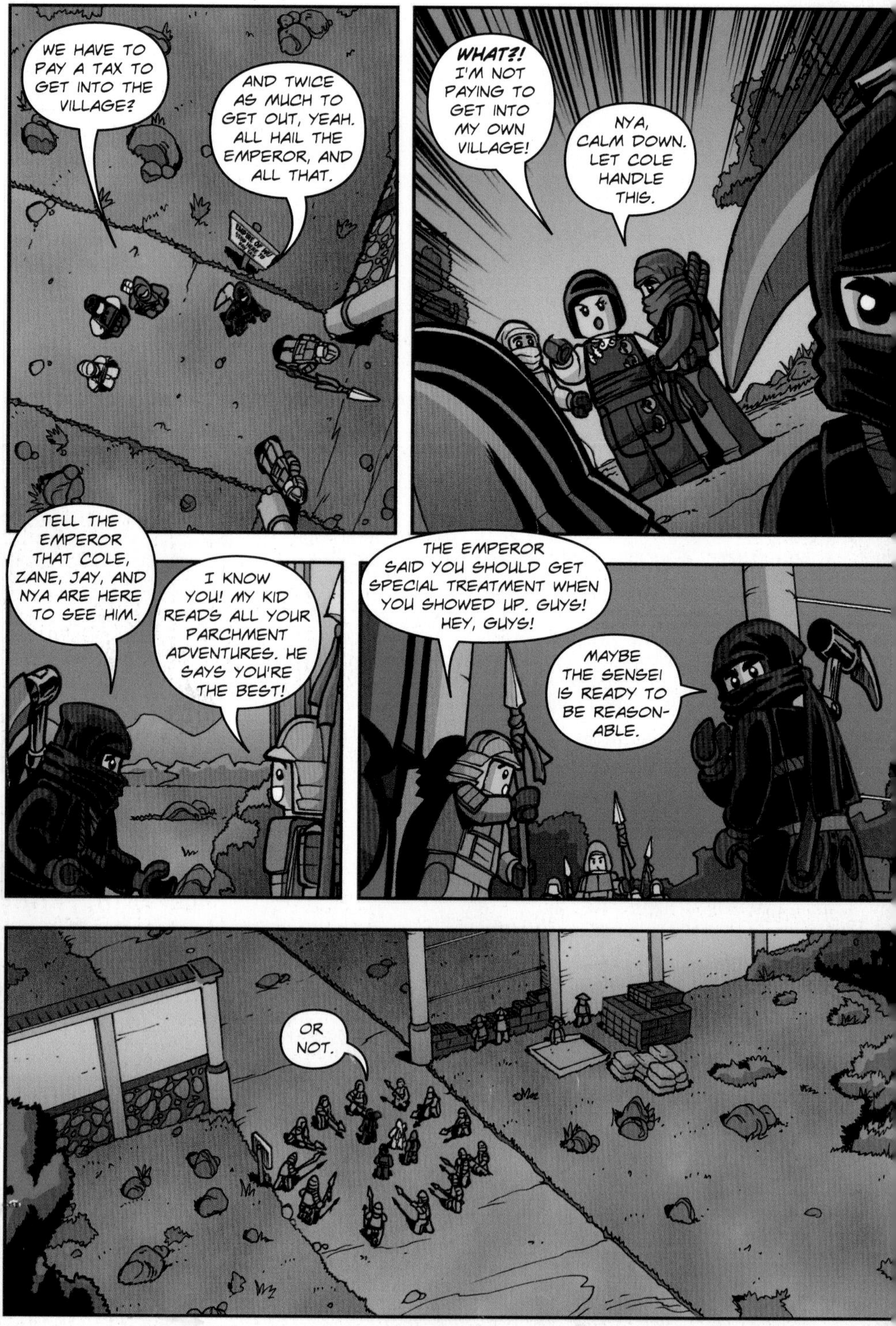
WE HAVE TO PAY A TAX TO GET INTO THE VILLAGE?
AND TWICE AS MUCH TO GET OUT, YEAH. ALL HAIL THE EMPEROR, AND ALL THAT.
WHAT?! I'M NOT PAYING TO GET INTO MY OWN VILLAGE!
NYA, CALM DOWN. LET COLE HANDLE THIS.
TELL THE EMPEROR THAT COLE, ZANE, JAY, AND NYA ARE HERE TO SEE HIM.
I KNOW YOU! MY KID READS ALL YOUR PARCHMENT ADVENTURES. HE SAYS YOU'RE THE BEST!
THE EMPEROR SAID YOU SHOULD GET SPECIAL TREATMENT WHEN YOU SHOWED UP. GUYS! HEY, GUYS!
MAYBE THE SENSEI IS READY TO BE REASON-ABLE.
OR NOT.

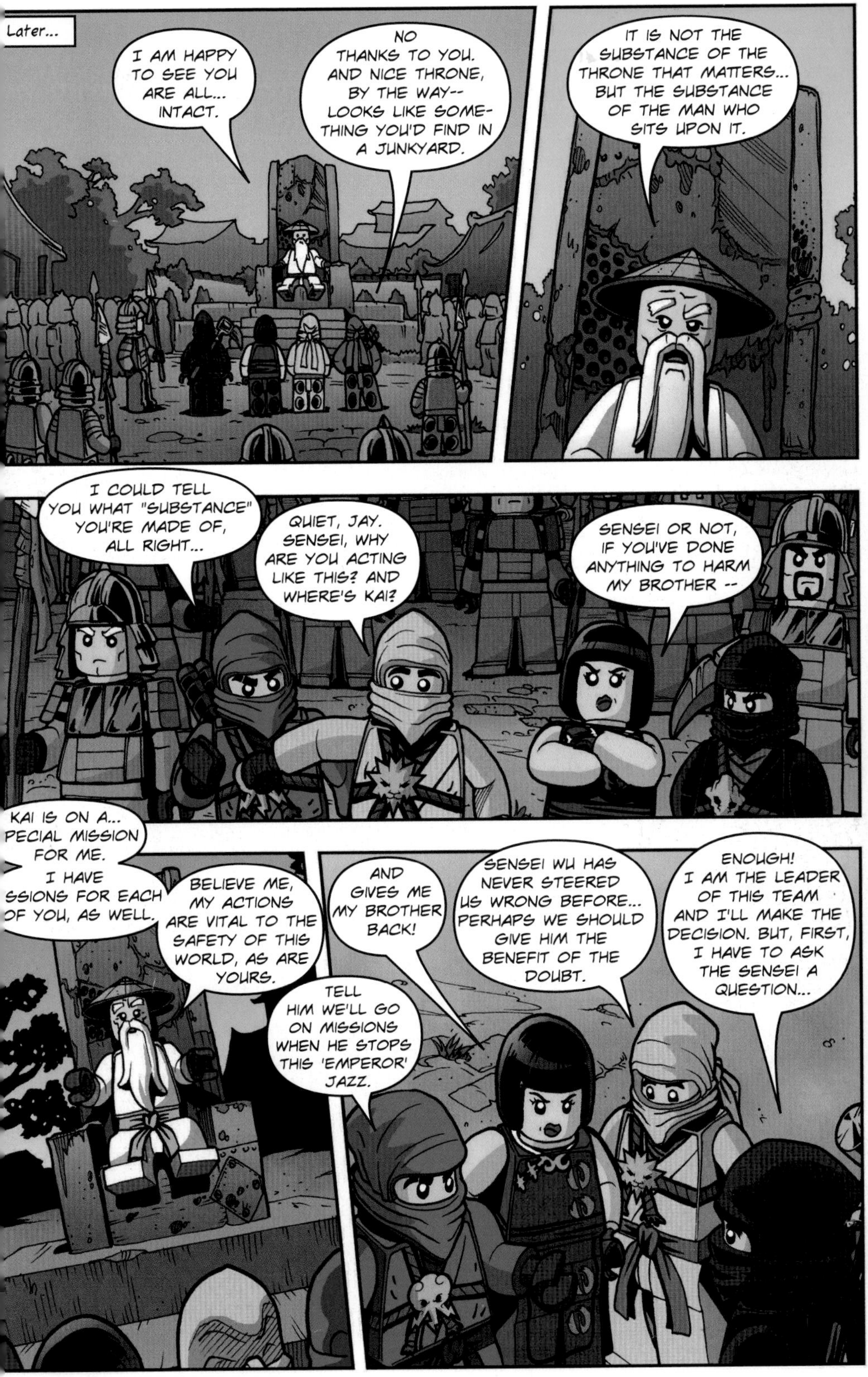

Later...
I AM HAPPY TO SEE YOU ARE ALL... INTACT.
NO THANKS TO YOU. AND NICE THRONE, BY THE WAY-- LOOKS LIKE SOME-THING YOU'D FIND IN A JUNKYARD.
IT IS NOT THE SUBSTANCE OF THE THRONE THAT MATTERS... BUT THE SUBSTANCE OF THE MAN WHO SITS UPON IT.
I COULD TELL YOU WHAT "SUBSTANCE" YOU'RE MADE OF, ALL RIGHT...
QUIET, JAY. SENSEI, WHY ARE YOU ACTING LIKE THIS? AND WHERE'S KAI?
SENSEI OR NOT, IF YOU'VE DONE ANYTHING TO HARM MY BROTHER --
KAI IS ON A... PECIAL MISSION FOR ME.
I HAVE SSIONS FOR EACH OF YOU, AS WELL.
BELIEVE ME, MY ACTIONS ARE VITAL TO THE SAFETY OF THIS WORLD, AS ARE YOURS.
TELL HIM WE'LL GO ON MISSIONS WHEN HE STOPS THIS 'EMPEROR' JAZZ.
AND GIVES ME MY BROTHER BACK!
SENSEI WU HAS NEVER STEERED US WRONG BEFORE... PERHAPS WE SHOULD GIVE HIM THE BENEFIT OF THE DOUBT.
ENOUGH! I AM THE LEADER OF THIS TEAM AND I'LL MAKE THE DECISION. BUT, FIRST, I HAVE TO ASK THE SENSEI A QUESTION...

CARE TO JOIN US FOR SOME TEA?

TEA? BAH! NEVER TOUCH THE STUFF.

HE DOESN'T TOUCH TEA?!

PERHAPS NYA WAS MORE CORRECT THAN SHE KNEW WHEN SHE SAID, 'SENSEI OR NOT ...' OUR TEACHER HAS NEVER TURNED DOWN A CUP OF TEA.

YOU THINK HE'S AN IMPOSTOR? WELL, WE'VE SEEN STRANGER THINGS. LIKE THIS LIST OF THINGS HE WANTS US TO GET...

THE SCALE OF AN ANGRY DRAGON... DUST FROM A RAGING RIVER... A SNOWBALL FROM THE GREAT DESERT... AND A SCROLL TAKEN FROM THE SAFEST PLACE IN NINJAGO.

THE SAFEST PLACE IN THIS WORLD? WHERE IS THAT?

THAT'S JUST ONE MYSTERY. DON'T FORGET WHO HE IS...

WHY HE WANTS THESE THINGS... AND MOST IMPORTANTLY, IF HE'S NOT SENSEI WU, WHERE IS THE REAL SENSEI?

24

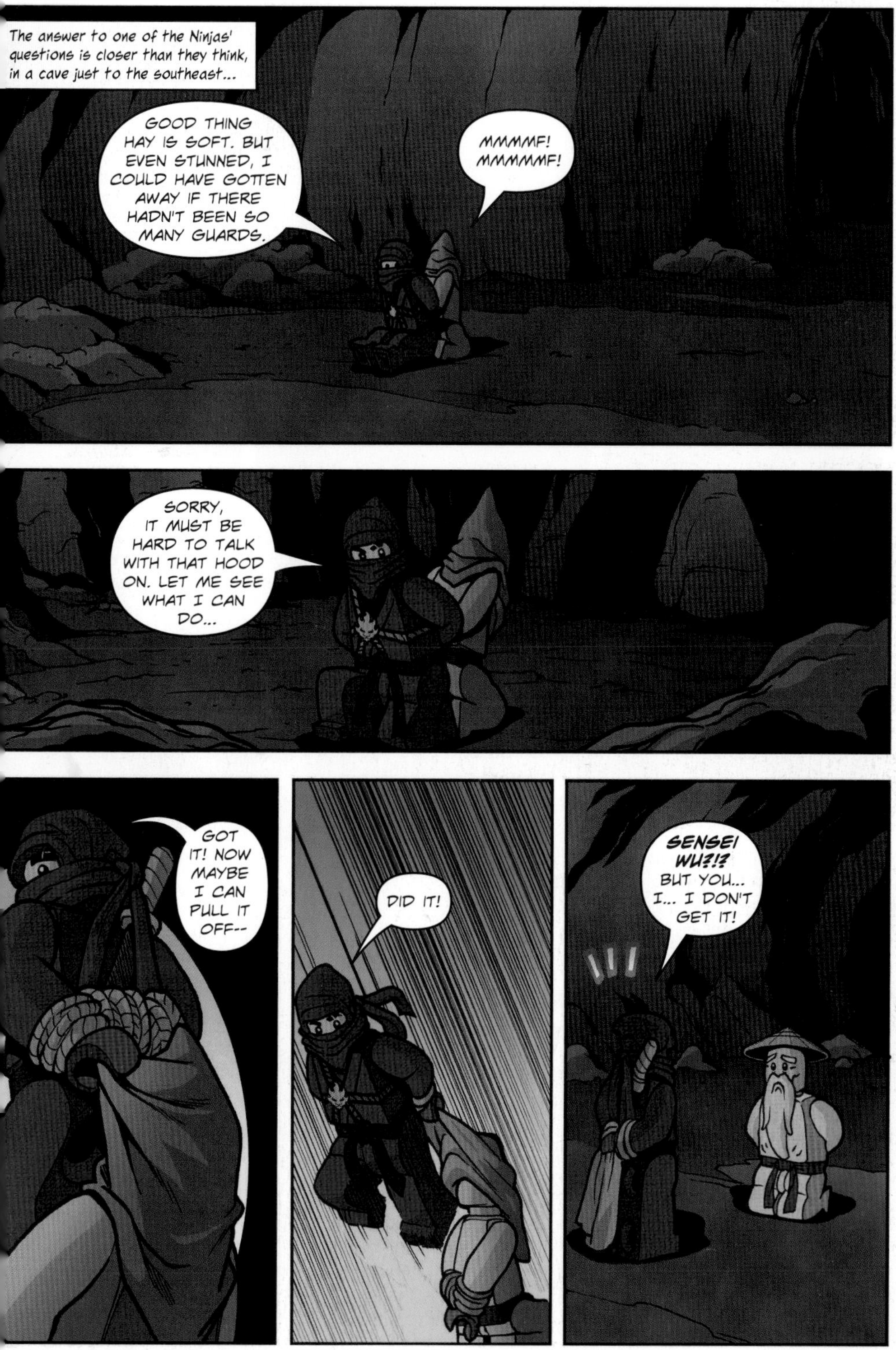
The answer to one of the Ninjas' questions is closer than they think, in a cave just to the southeast...
GOOD THING HAY IS SOFT. BUT EVEN STUNNED, I COULD HAVE GOTTEN AWAY IF THERE HADN'T BEEN SO MANY GUARDS.
MMMMF! MMMMMF!
SORRY, IT MUST BE HARD TO TALK WITH THAT HOOD ON. LET ME SEE WHAT I CAN DO...
GOT IT! NOW MAYBE I CAN PULL IT OFF--
DID IT!
SENSEI WU?!? BUT YOU... I... I DON'T GET IT!

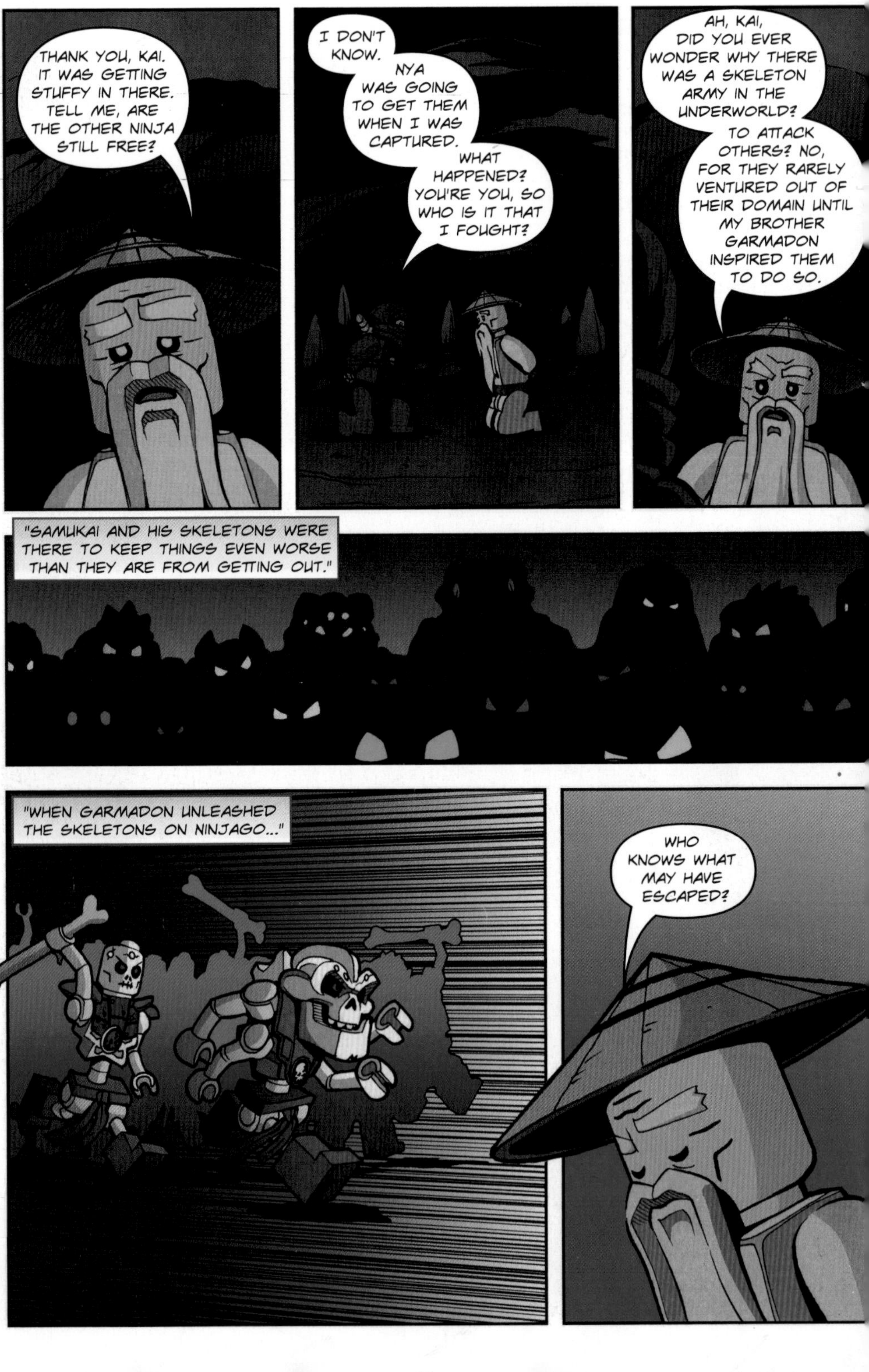
THANK YOU, KAI. IT WAS GETTING STUFFY IN THERE. TELL ME, ARE THE OTHER NINJA STILL FREE?
I DON'T KNOW.
NYA WAS GOING TO GET THEM WHEN I WAS CAPTURED.
WHAT HAPPENED? YOU'RE YOU, SO WHO IS IT THAT I FOUGHT?
AH, KAI, DID YOU EVER WONDER WHY THERE WAS A SKELETON ARMY IN THE UNDERWORLD?
TO ATTACK OTHERS? NO, FOR THEY RARELY VENTURED OUT OF THEIR DOMAIN UNTIL MY BROTHER GARMADON INSPIRED THEM TO DO SO.
"SAMUKAI AND HIS SKELETONS WERE THERE TO KEEP THINGS EVEN WORSE THAN THEY ARE FROM GETTING OUT."
"WHEN GARMADON UNLEASHED THE SKELETONS ON NINJAGO..."
WHO KNOWS WHAT MAY HAVE ESCAPED?

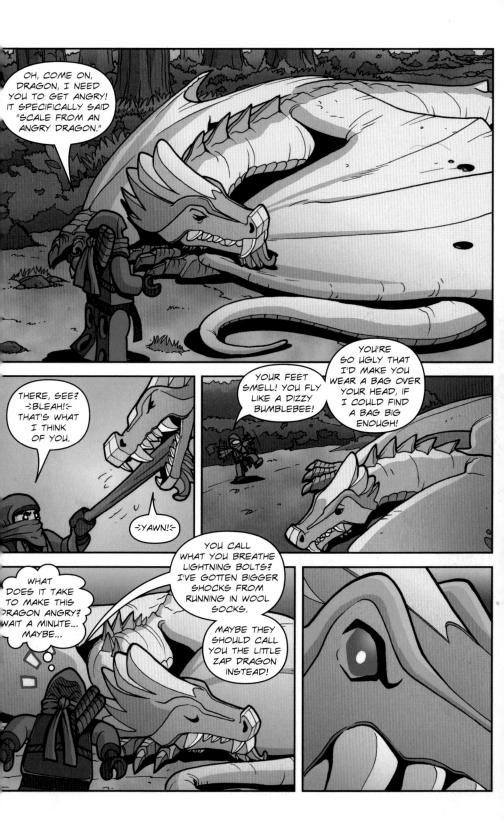

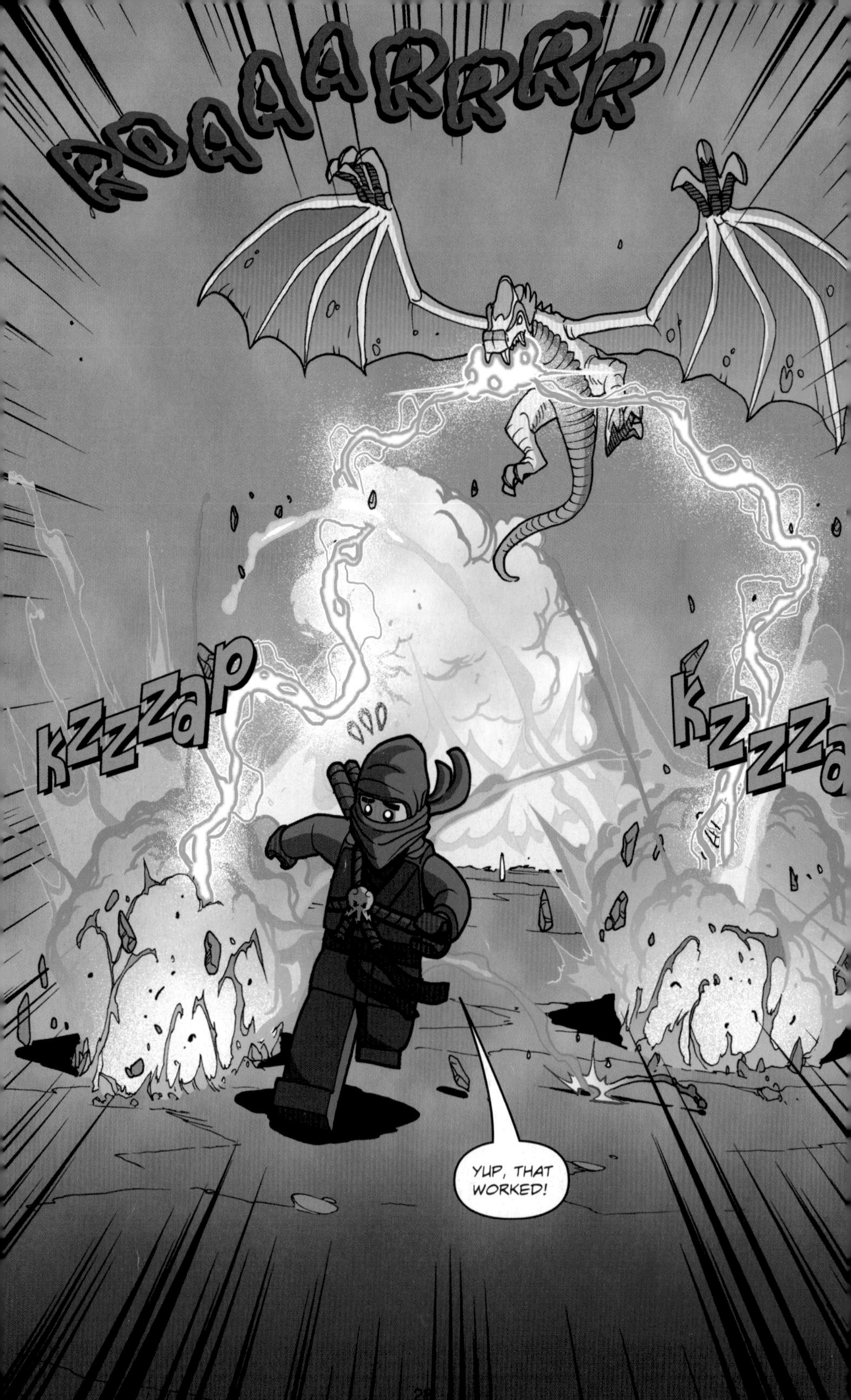
ROAAARRRR
KZZZAP
KZZZA
YUP, THAT WORKED!

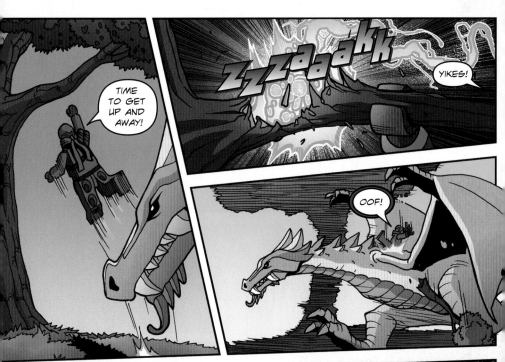

TIME TO GET UP AND AWAY!

zzzaaakk

YIKES!

OOF!

THIS SHOULD DO IT.

ONE SCALE FROM AN ANGRY DRAGON... PIECE OF CAKE!

UMMM... I MEAN... SEE, IT'S LIKE THIS...

BYE!

KZZZAAKK

KA-BAMMM

BOY, WHEN HE GETS ANGRY, HE REALLY GETS ANGRY!

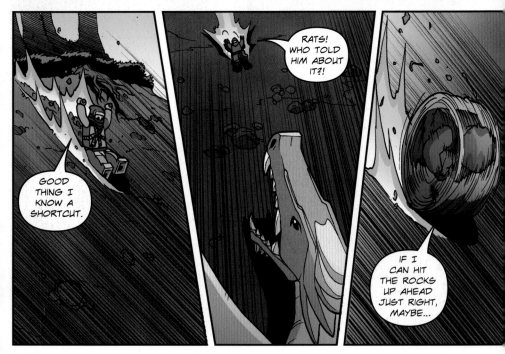

GOOD THING I KNOW A SHORTCUT.

RATS! WHO TOLD HIM ABOUT IT?!

IF I CAN HIT THE ROCKS UP AHEAD JUST RIGHT, MAYBE...

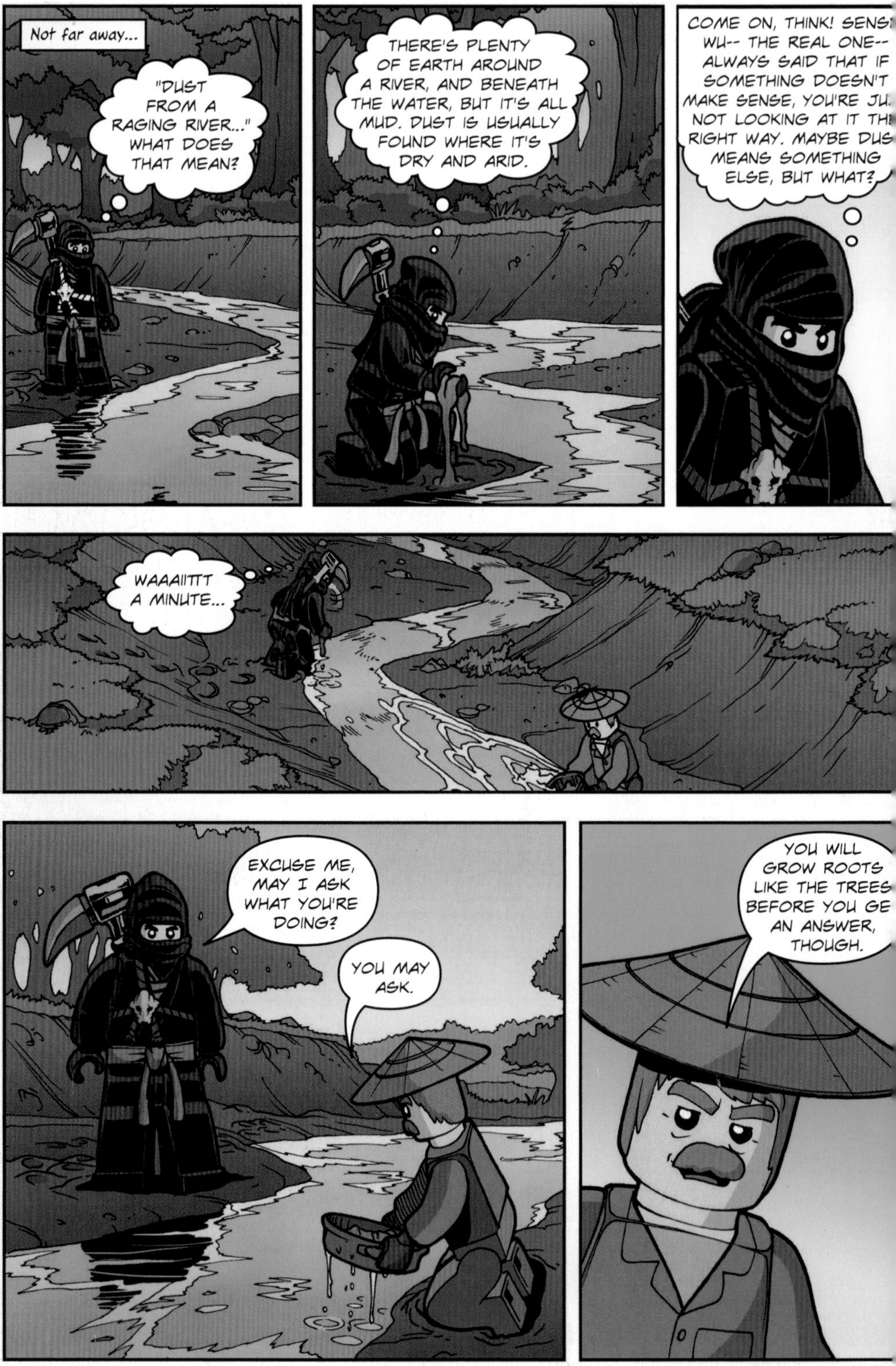
Not far away...
"DUST FROM A RAGING RIVER..." WHAT DOES THAT MEAN?
THERE'S PLENTY OF EARTH AROUND A RIVER, AND BENEATH THE WATER, BUT IT'S ALL MUD. DUST IS USUALLY FOUND WHERE IT'S DRY AND ARID.
COME ON, THINK! SENS WU-- THE REAL ONE-- ALWAYS SAID THAT IF SOMETHING DOESN'T MAKE SENSE, YOU'RE JU NOT LOOKING AT IT TH RIGHT WAY. MAYBE DUS MEANS SOMETHING ELSE, BUT WHAT?
WAAAIITTT A MINUTE...
EXCUSE ME, MAY I ASK WHAT YOU'RE DOING?
YOU MAY ASK.
YOU WILL GROW ROOTS LIKE THE TREES BEFORE YOU GE AN ANSWER, THOUGH.

WELL, LET'S SEE. YOU EITHER REALLY WANT TO MAKE SURE YOUR COOK PAN IS CLEAN...

OR YOU'RE PANNING FOR GOLD.

AH, A WISE NINJA. HOW RARE. YES, I COME HERE TO SEARCH THE WATERS FOR GOLD DUST, BUT IT SEEMS TODAY I HAVE FOUND SOMETHING ELSE.

A THIEF!

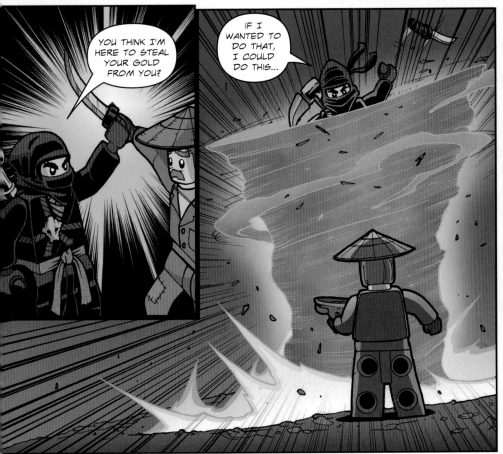

YOU THINK I'M HERE TO STEAL YOUR GOLD FROM YOU?

IF I WANTED TO DO THAT, I COULD DO THIS...

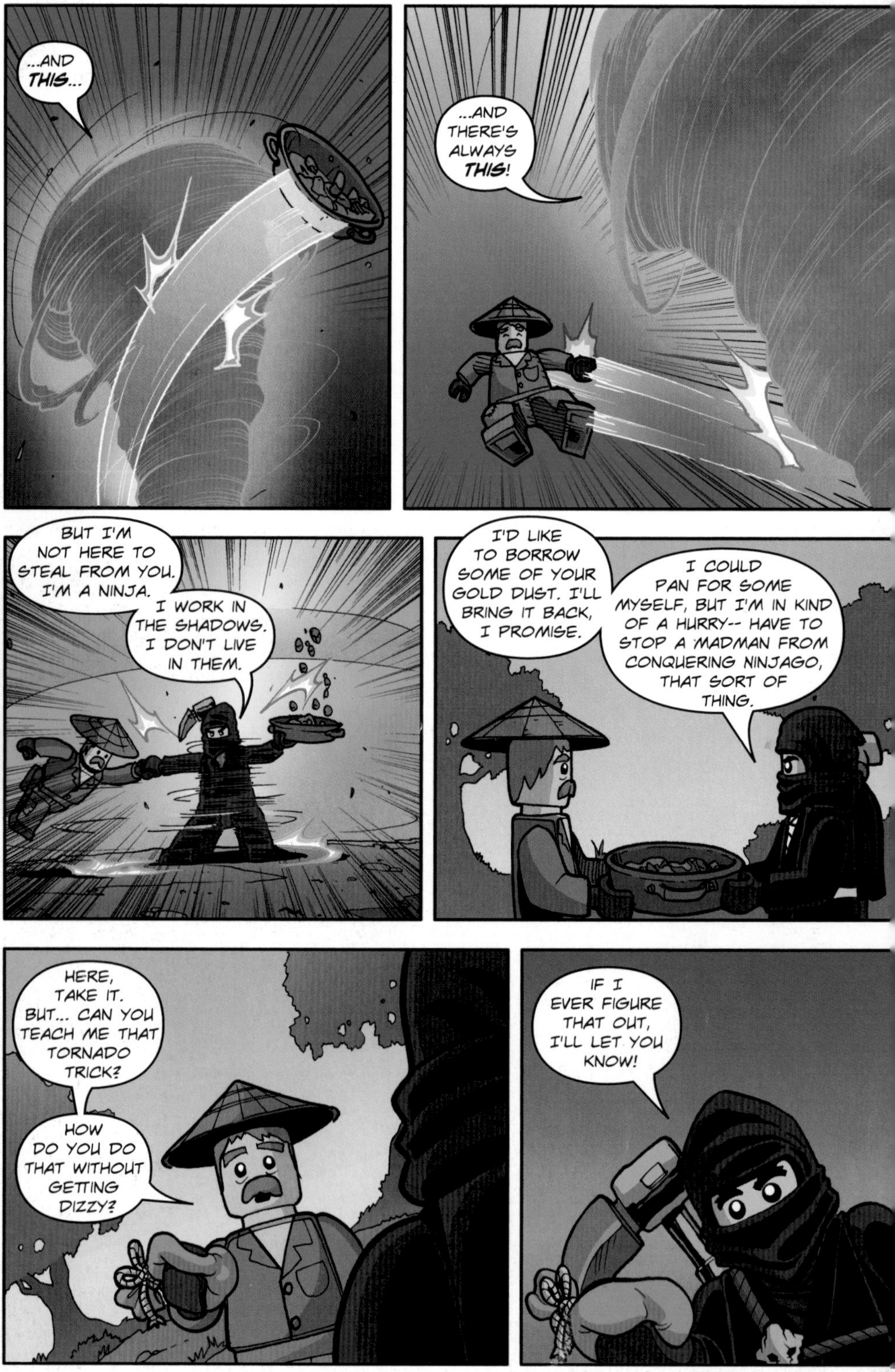
...AND THIS...
...AND THERE'S ALWAYS THIS!
BUT I'M NOT HERE TO STEAL FROM YOU. I'M A NINJA.
I WORK IN THE SHADOWS. I DON'T LIVE IN THEM.
I'D LIKE TO BORROW SOME OF YOUR GOLD DUST. I'LL BRING IT BACK, I PROMISE.
I COULD PAN FOR SOME MYSELF, BUT I'M IN KIND OF A HURRY-- HAVE TO STOP A MADMAN FROM CONQUERING NINJAGO, THAT SORT OF THING.
HERE, TAKE IT. BUT... CAN YOU TEACH ME THAT TORNADO TRICK?
HOW DO YOU DO THAT WITHOUT GETTING DIZZY?
IF I EVER FIGURE THAT OUT, I'LL LET YOU KNOW!

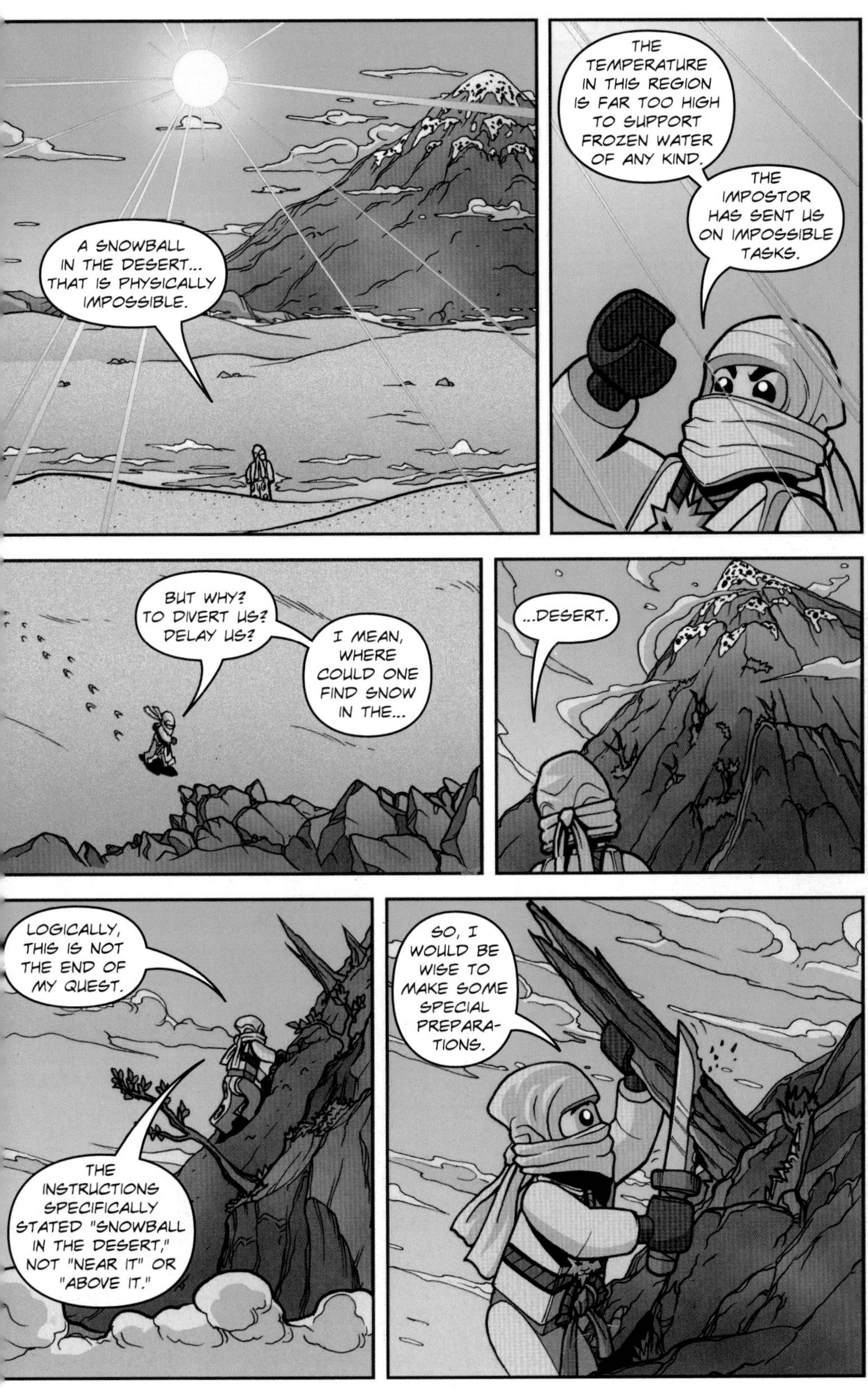
A SNOWBALL IN THE DESERT... THAT IS PHYSICALLY IMPOSSIBLE.
THE TEMPERATURE IN THIS REGION IS FAR TOO HIGH TO SUPPORT FROZEN WATER OF ANY KIND.
THE IMPOSTOR HAS SENT US ON IMPOSSIBLE TASKS.
BUT WHY? TO DIVERT US? DELAY US?
I MEAN, WHERE COULD ONE FIND SNOW IN THE...
...DESERT.
LOGICALLY, THIS IS NOT THE END OF MY QUEST.
THE INSTRUCTIONS SPECIFICALLY STATED "SNOWBALL IN THE DESERT," NOT "NEAR IT" OR "ABOVE IT."
SO, I WOULD BE WISE TO MAKE SOME SPECIAL PREPARA-TIONS.

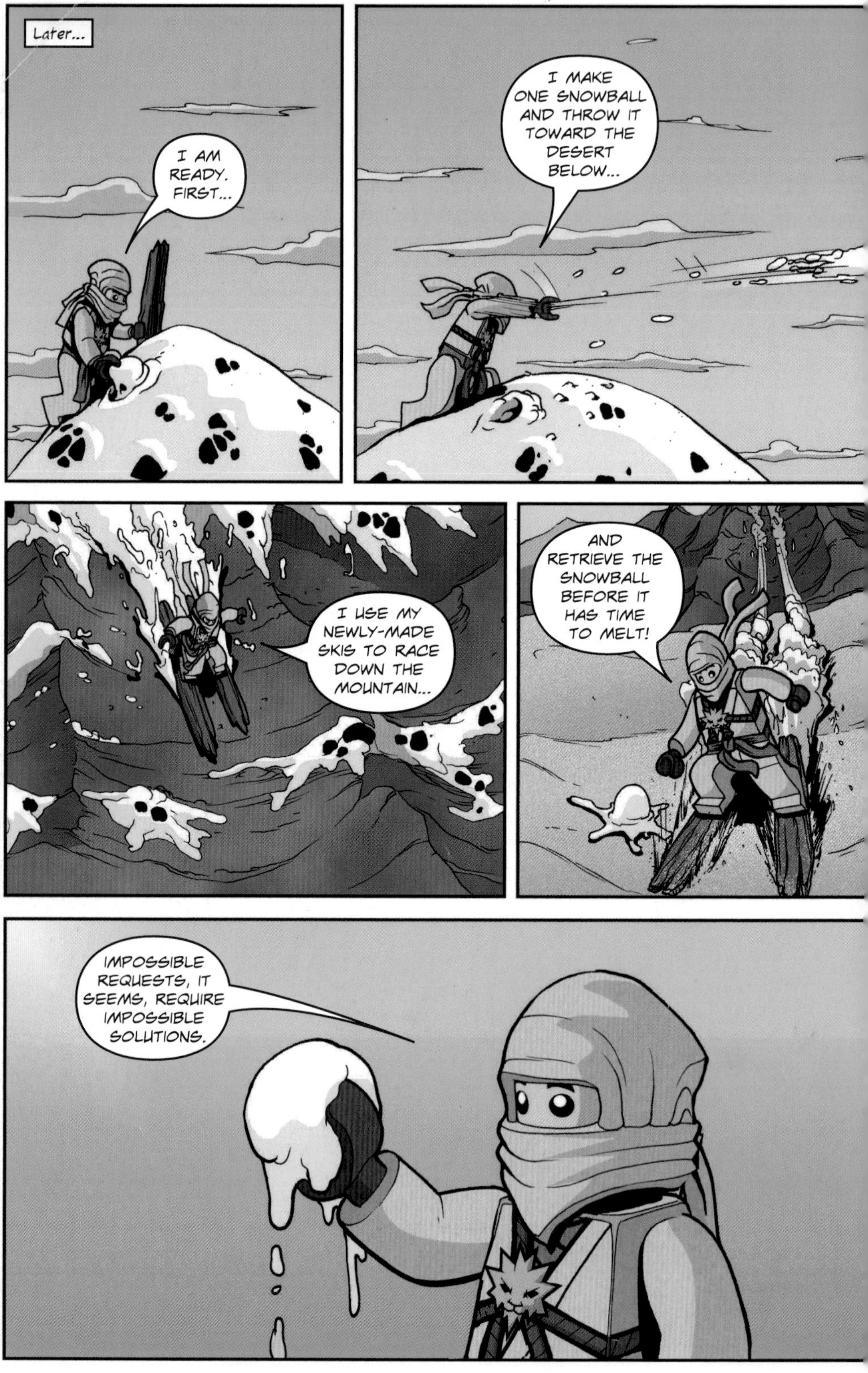

Later...
I AM READY. FIRST...
I MAKE ONE SNOWBALL AND THROW IT TOWARD THE DESERT BELOW...
I USE MY NEWLY-MADE SKIS TO RACE DOWN THE MOUNTAIN...
AND RETRIEVE THE SNOWBALL BEFORE IT HAS TIME TO MELT!
IMPOSSIBLE REQUESTS, IT SEEMS, REQUIRE IMPOSSIBLE SOLUTIONS.

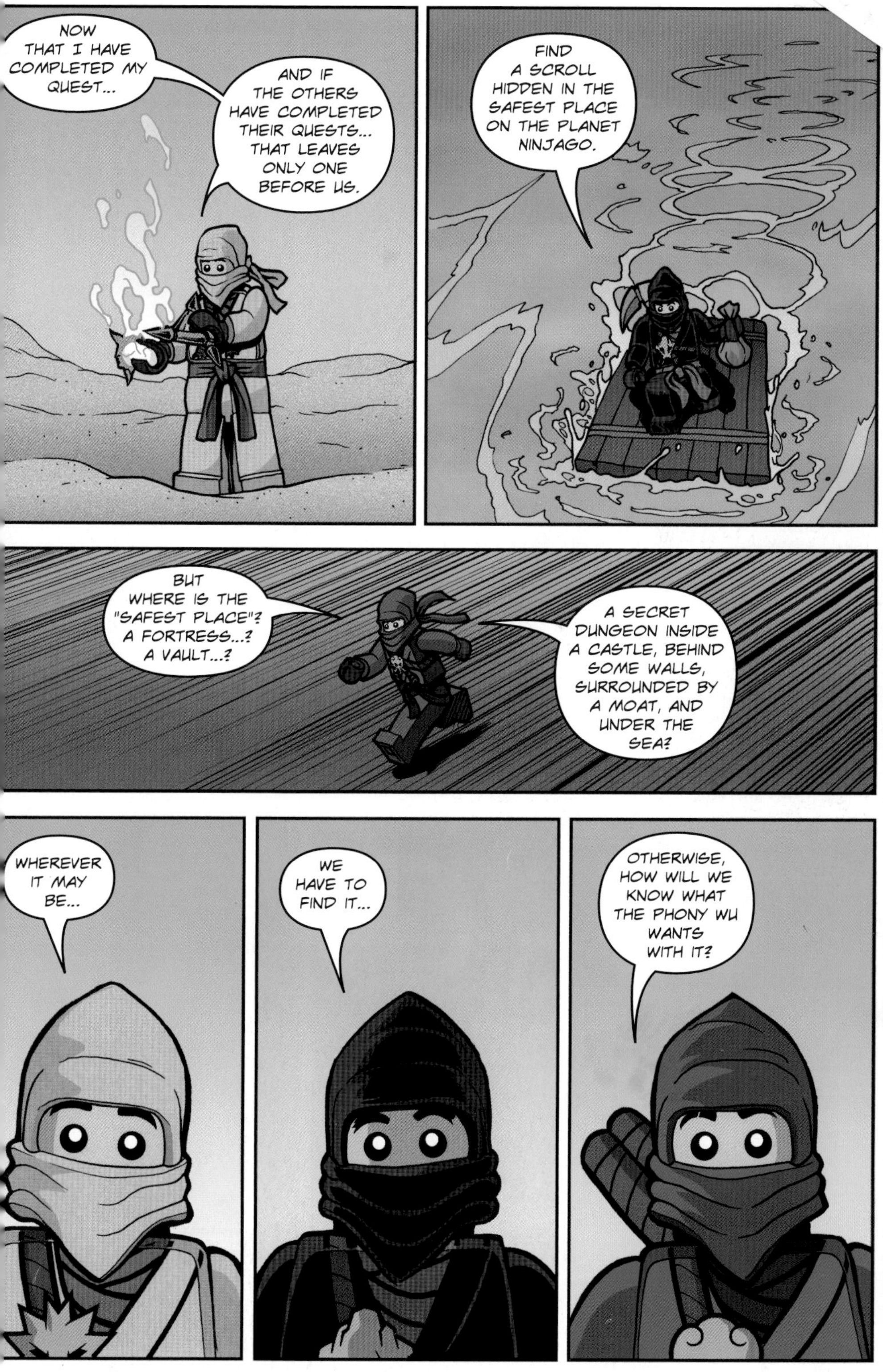
NOW THAT I HAVE COMPLETED MY QUEST...
AND IF THE OTHERS HAVE COMPLETED THEIR QUESTS... THAT LEAVES ONLY ONE BEFORE US.
FIND A SCROLL HIDDEN IN THE SAFEST PLACE ON THE PLANET NINJAGO.
BUT WHERE IS THE "SAFEST PLACE"? A FORTRESS...? A VAULT...?
A SECRET DUNGEON INSIDE A CASTLE, BEHIND SOME WALLS, SURROUNDED BY A MOAT, AND UNDER THE SEA?
WHEREVER IT MAY BE...
WE HAVE TO FIND IT...
OTHERWISE, HOW WILL WE KNOW WHAT THE PHONY WU WANTS WITH IT?

IT BELONGS TO A SPECIES SO OLD THAT EVEN ITS NAME IS LOST TO HISTORY.

"In its natural form, it is little more than smoke. It survives by taking the form of others, stealing its new shape from the memories of those around it."

"In this case, it no doubt got its inspiration from my brother, Garmadon, who spent so much of his time plotting revenge on me," says Sensei Wu.

"Those memories of me were all it needed to make a change."

BUT WHY WOULDN'T IT JUST MAKE ITSELF LOOK LIKE GARMADON?

GARMADON WAS POWERFUL, YES, BUT FEARED AND HATED AS WELL.

SO, IT CAPTURED YOU, AND FAKED THE WAGON ACCIDENT.

THAT WAY, IF IT GOT ANY DETAILS WRONG OR "SENSEI WU" SEEMED TO BE ACTING STRANGE, WE WOULD BLAME IT ON THE BLOW TO THE HEAD. INCREDIBLE.

TO ACHIEVE ITS ENDS, THIS THING NEEDS TO BE HONORED AND ADMIRED.

IT NEEDED TO BECOME SOMEONE OTHERS WOULD TRUST.

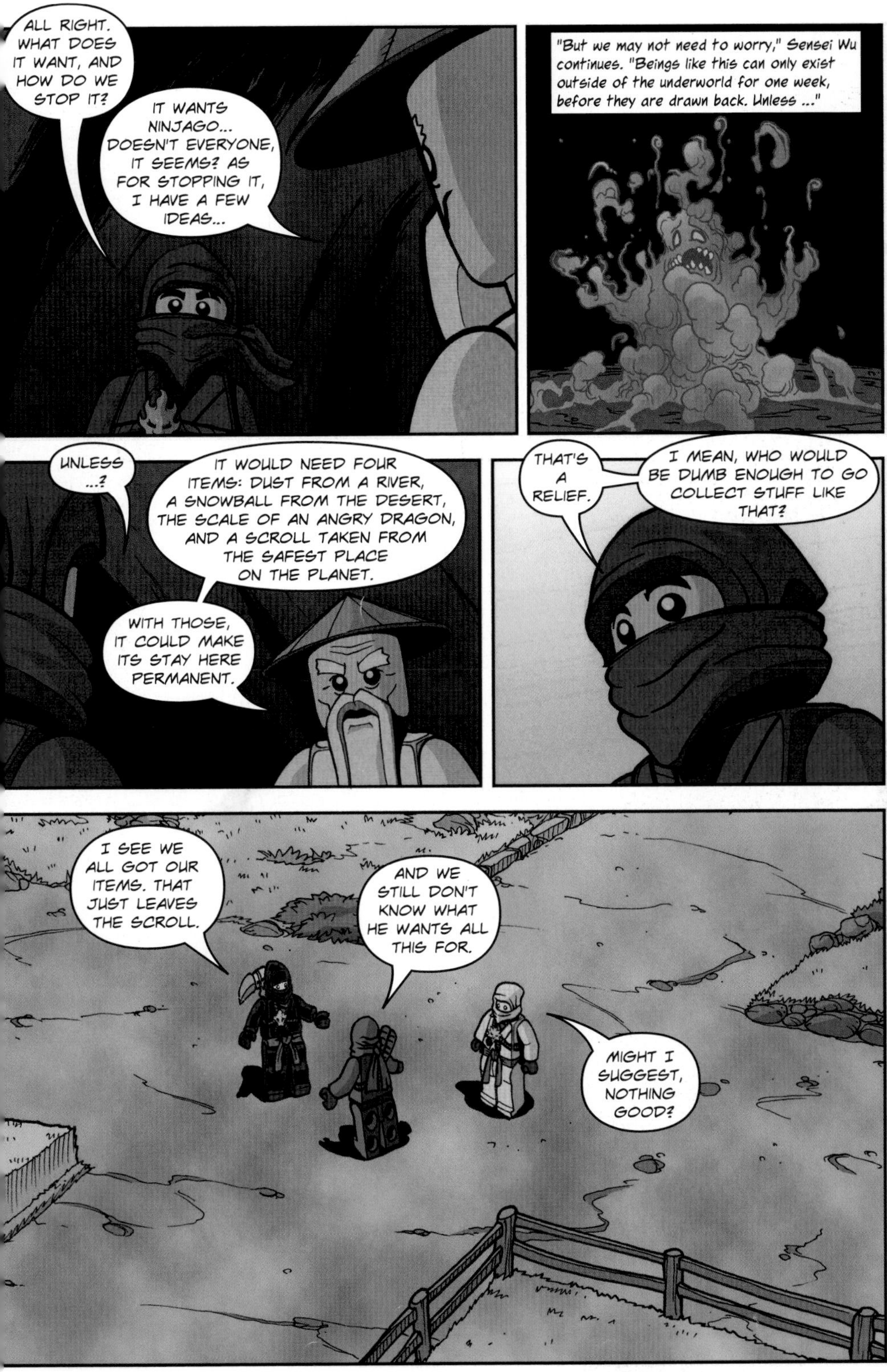
ALL RIGHT. WHAT DOES IT WANT, AND HOW DO WE STOP IT?
IT WANTS NINJAGO... DOESN'T EVERYONE, IT SEEMS? AS FOR STOPPING IT, I HAVE A FEW IDEAS...
"But we may not need to worry," Sensei Wu continues. "Beings like this can only exist outside of the underworld for one week, before they are drawn back. Unless ..."
UNLESS ...?
IT WOULD NEED FOUR ITEMS: DUST FROM A RIVER, A SNOWBALL FROM THE DESERT, THE SCALE OF AN ANGRY DRAGON, AND A SCROLL TAKEN FROM THE SAFEST PLACE ON THE PLANET.
WITH THOSE, IT COULD MAKE ITS STAY HERE PERMANENT.
THAT'S A RELIEF.
I MEAN, WHO WOULD BE DUMB ENOUGH TO GO COLLECT STUFF LIKE THAT?
I SEE WE ALL GOT OUR ITEMS. THAT JUST LEAVES THE SCROLL.
AND WE STILL DON'T KNOW WHAT HE WANTS ALL THIS FOR.
MIGHT I SUGGEST, NOTHING GOOD?

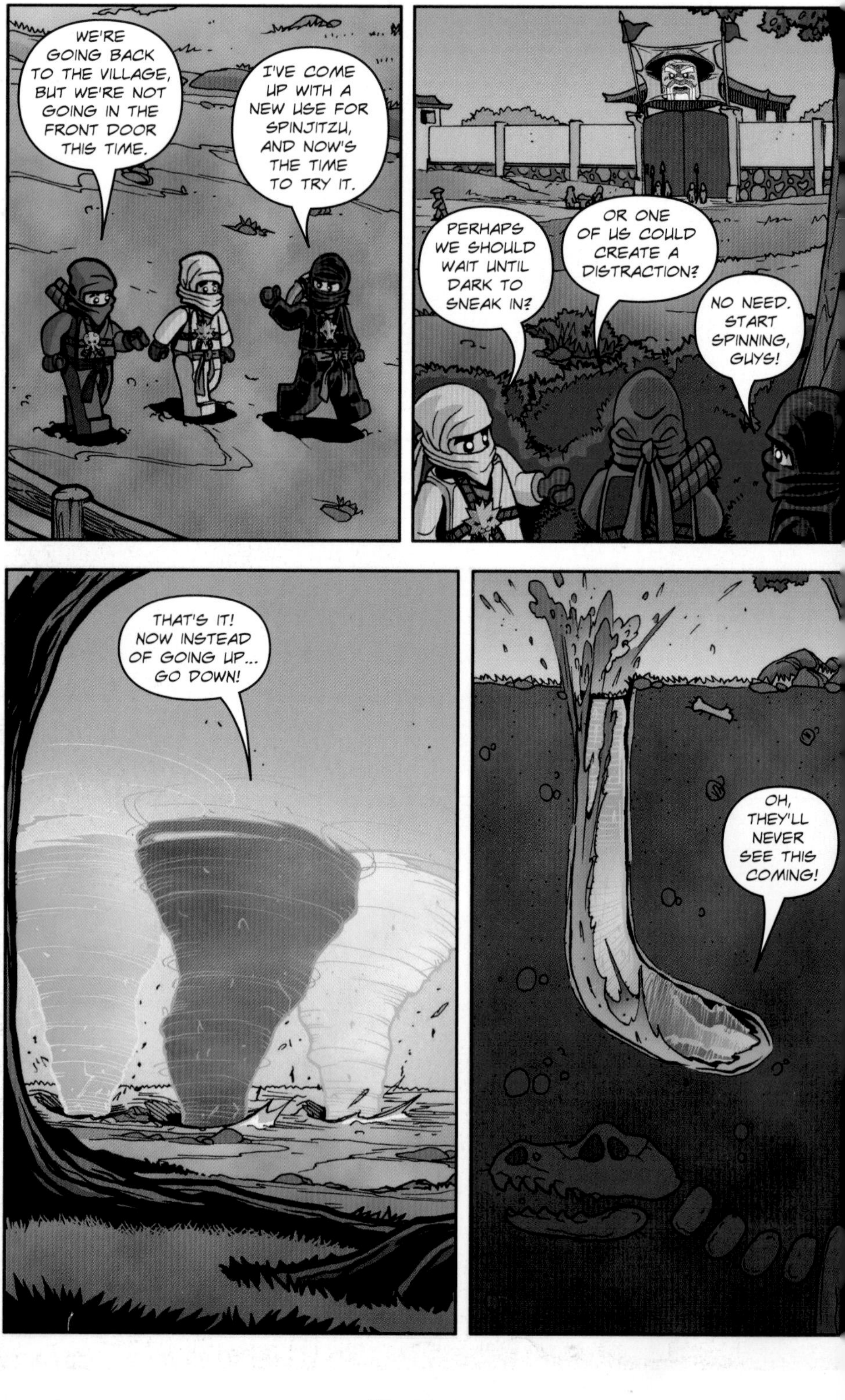
WE'RE GOING BACK TO THE VILLAGE, BUT WE'RE NOT GOING IN THE FRONT DOOR THIS TIME.
I'VE COME UP WITH A NEW USE FOR SPINJITZU, AND NOW'S THE TIME TO TRY IT.
PERHAPS WE SHOULD WAIT UNTIL DARK TO SNEAK IN?
OR ONE OF US COULD CREATE A DISTRACTION?
NO NEED. START SPINNING, GUYS!
THAT'S IT! NOW INSTEAD OF GOING UP... GO DOWN!
OH, THEY'LL NEVER SEE THIS COMING!

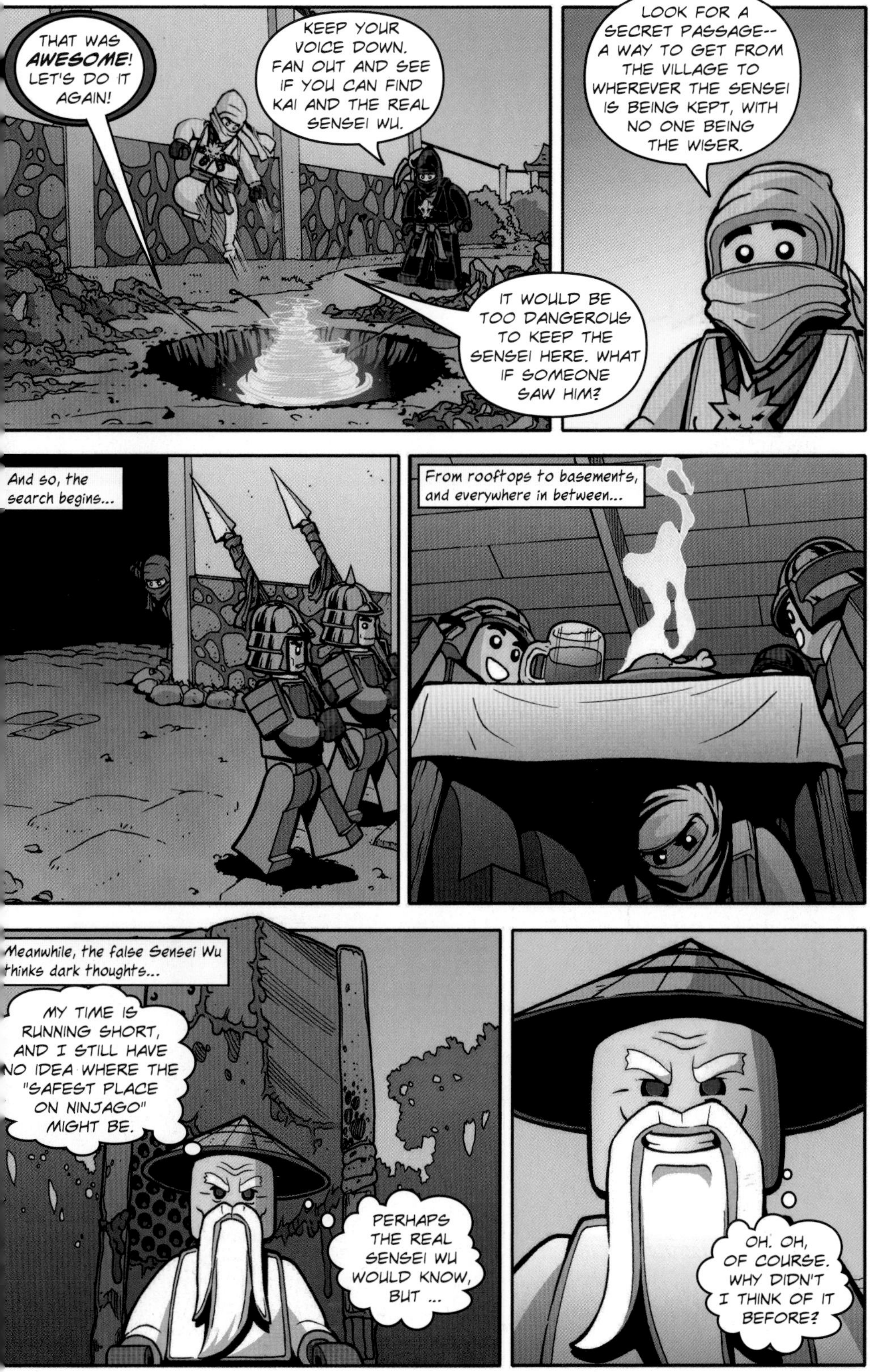
THAT WAS **AWESOME**! LET'S DO IT AGAIN!
KEEP YOUR VOICE DOWN. FAN OUT AND SEE IF YOU CAN FIND KAI AND THE REAL SENSEI WU.
IT WOULD BE TOO DANGEROUS TO KEEP THE SENSEI HERE. WHAT IF SOMEONE SAW HIM?
LOOK FOR A SECRET PASSAGE-- A WAY TO GET FROM THE VILLAGE TO WHEREVER THE SENSEI IS BEING KEPT, WITH NO ONE BEING THE WISER.
And so, the search begins...
From rooftops to basements, and everywhere in between...
Meanwhile, the false Sensei Wu thinks dark thoughts...
MY TIME IS RUNNING SHORT, AND I STILL HAVE NO IDEA WHERE THE "SAFEST PLACE ON NINJAGO" MIGHT BE.
PERHAPS THE REAL SENSEI WU WOULD KNOW, BUT ...
OH. OH, OF COURSE. WHY DIDN'T I THINK OF IT BEFORE?

VERY CLEVER, THOUGH I DO NOT KNOW HOW YOU MANAGED IT.

BUT YOU FORGET...

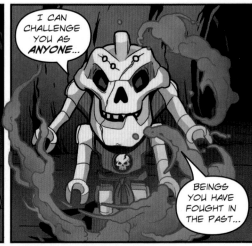

I CAN CHALLENGE YOU AS *ANYONE*...

BEINGS YOU HAVE FOUGHT IN THE PAST...

OR *FEARED* IN THE PAST!

I CAN BE A TRUSTED ALLY...

A BENEVOLENT MENTOR...

OR EVEN A BELOVED MEMBER OF YOUR FAMILY!

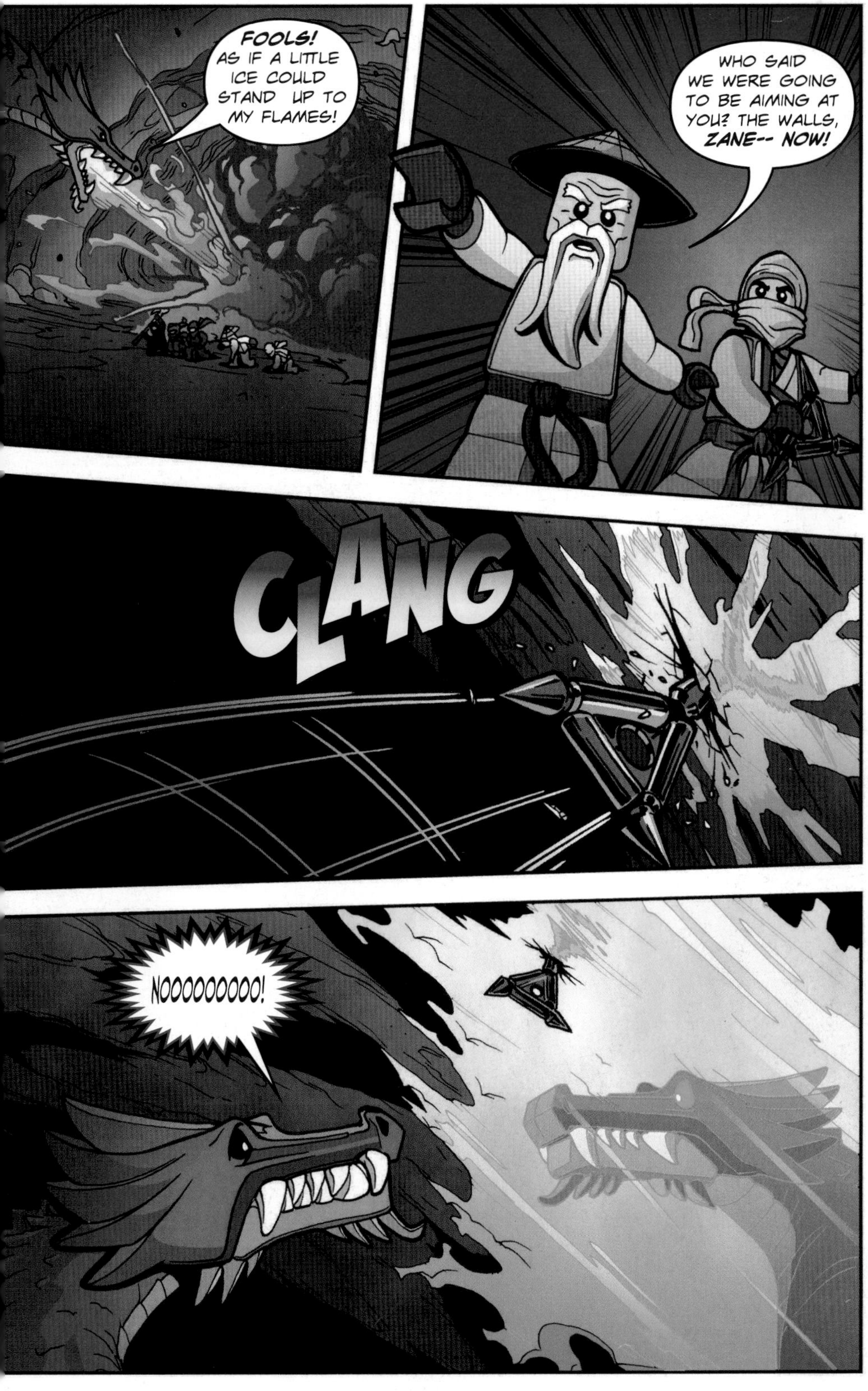
FOOLS! AS IF A LITTLE ICE COULD STAND UP TO MY FLAMES!
WHO SAID WE WERE GOING TO BE AIMING AT YOU? THE WALLS, ZANE-- NOW!
CLANG
NOOOOOOOOO!

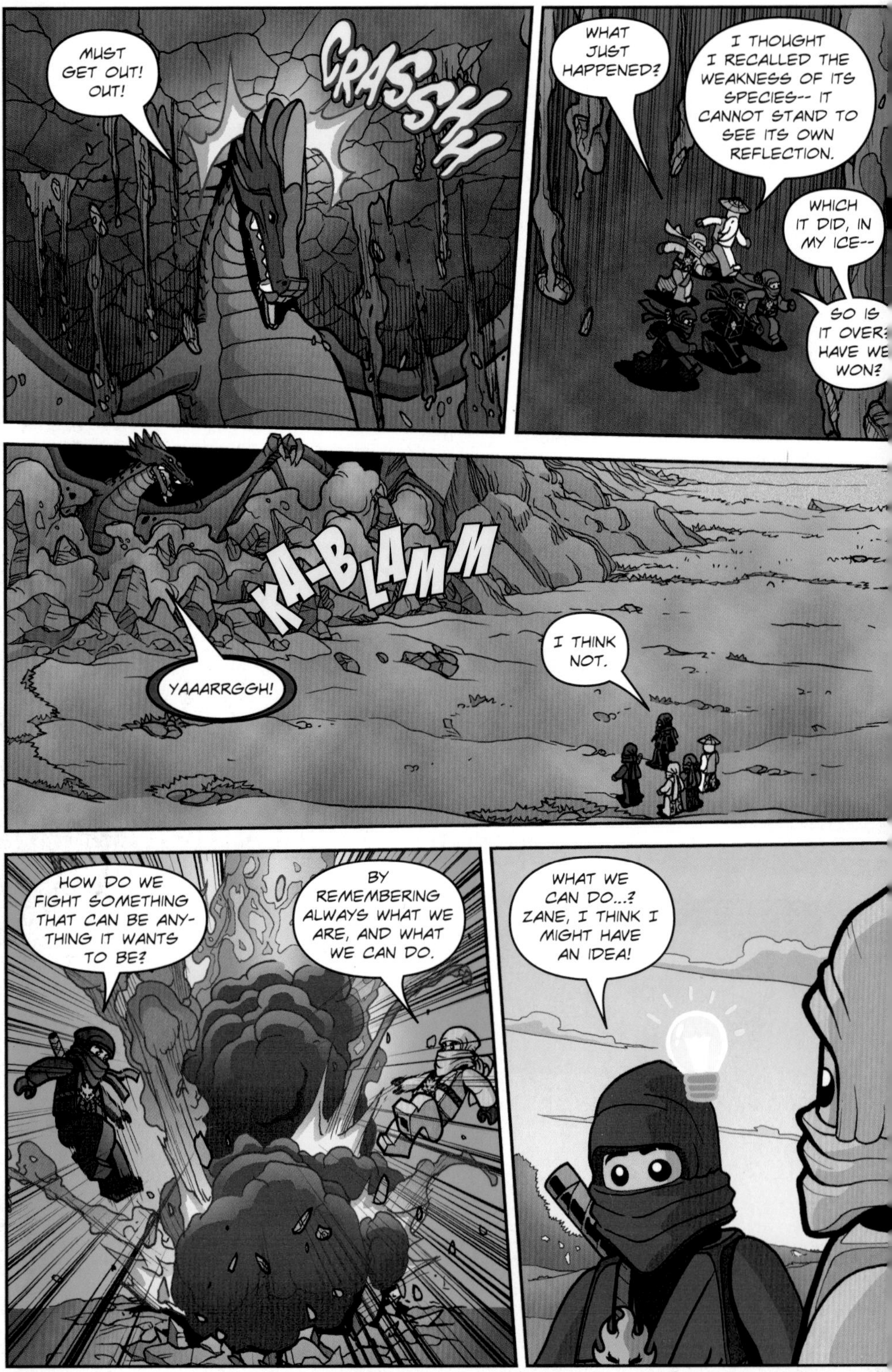
MUST GET OUT! OUT!
CRASSHH
WHAT JUST HAPPENED?
I THOUGHT I RECALLED THE WEAKNESS OF ITS SPECIES-- IT CANNOT STAND TO SEE ITS OWN REFLECTION.
WHICH IT DID, IN MY ICE--
SO IS IT OVER? HAVE WE WON?
KA-BLAMM
YAAARRGGH!
I THINK NOT.
HOW DO WE FIGHT SOMETHING THAT CAN BE ANY-THING IT WANTS TO BE?
BY REMEMBERING ALWAYS WHAT WE ARE, AND WHAT WE CAN DO.
WHAT WE CAN DO...? ZANE, I THINK I MIGHT HAVE AN IDEA!

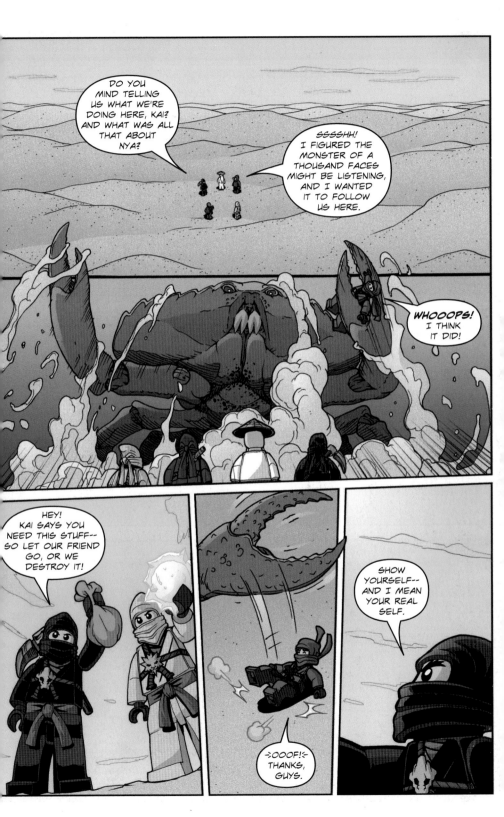

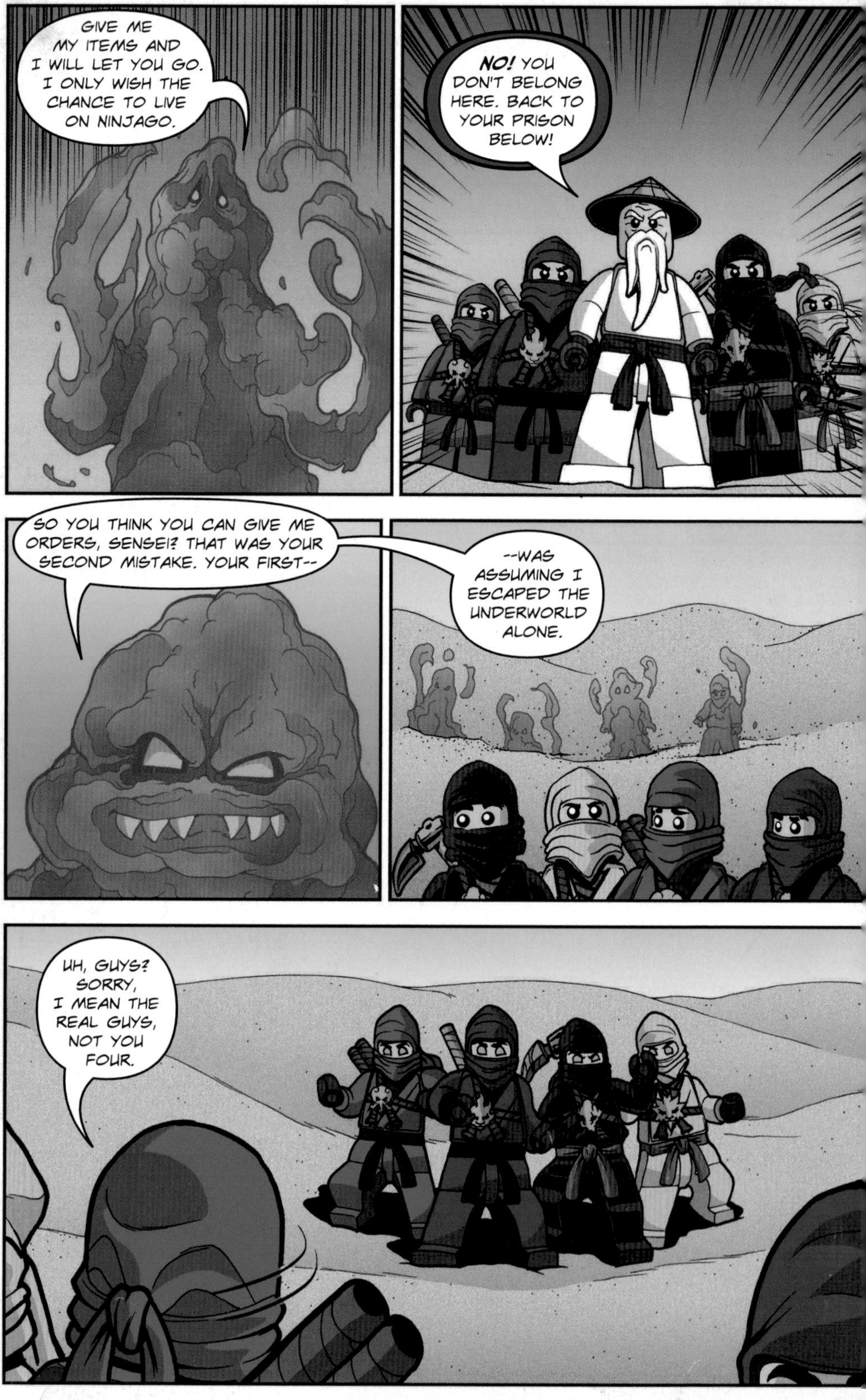
GIVE ME MY ITEMS AND I WILL LET YOU GO. I ONLY WISH THE CHANCE TO LIVE ON NINJAGO.
NO! YOU DON'T BELONG HERE. BACK TO YOUR PRISON BELOW!
SO YOU THINK YOU CAN GIVE ME ORDERS, SENSEI? THAT WAS YOUR SECOND MISTAKE. YOUR FIRST--
--WAS ASSUMING I ESCAPED THE UNDERWORLD ALONE.
UH, GUYS? SORRY, I MEAN THE REAL GUYS, NOT YOU FOUR.

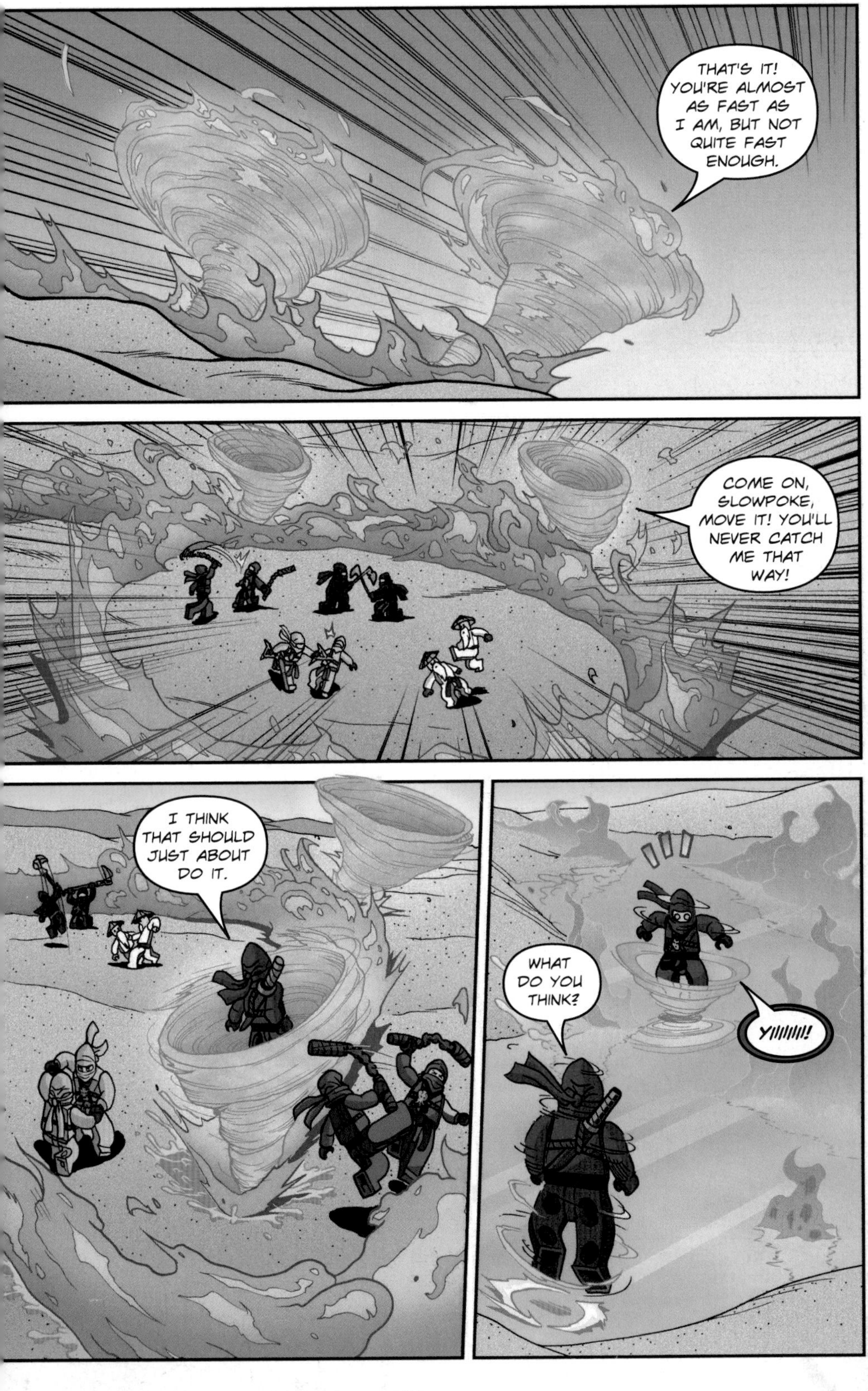
THAT'S IT! YOU'RE ALMOST AS FAST AS I AM, BUT NOT QUITE FAST ENOUGH.
COME ON, SLOWPOKE, MOVE IT! YOU'LL NEVER CATCH ME THAT WAY!
I THINK THAT SHOULD JUST ABOUT DO IT.
WHAT DO YOU THINK?
YIIIIIII!

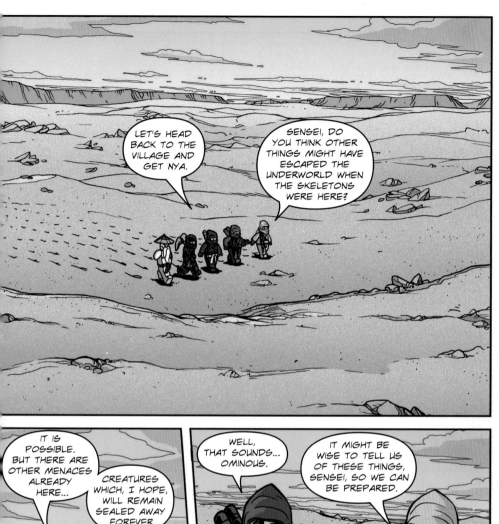

The End